Cover art by Damián V.

Cover design by MiblArt

Map by Maarten DeWekker

SHIELD OF SHADOW

• A SCEPTER AND CROWN NOVELLA •

C. F. E. BLACK

HILLCITY PRESS

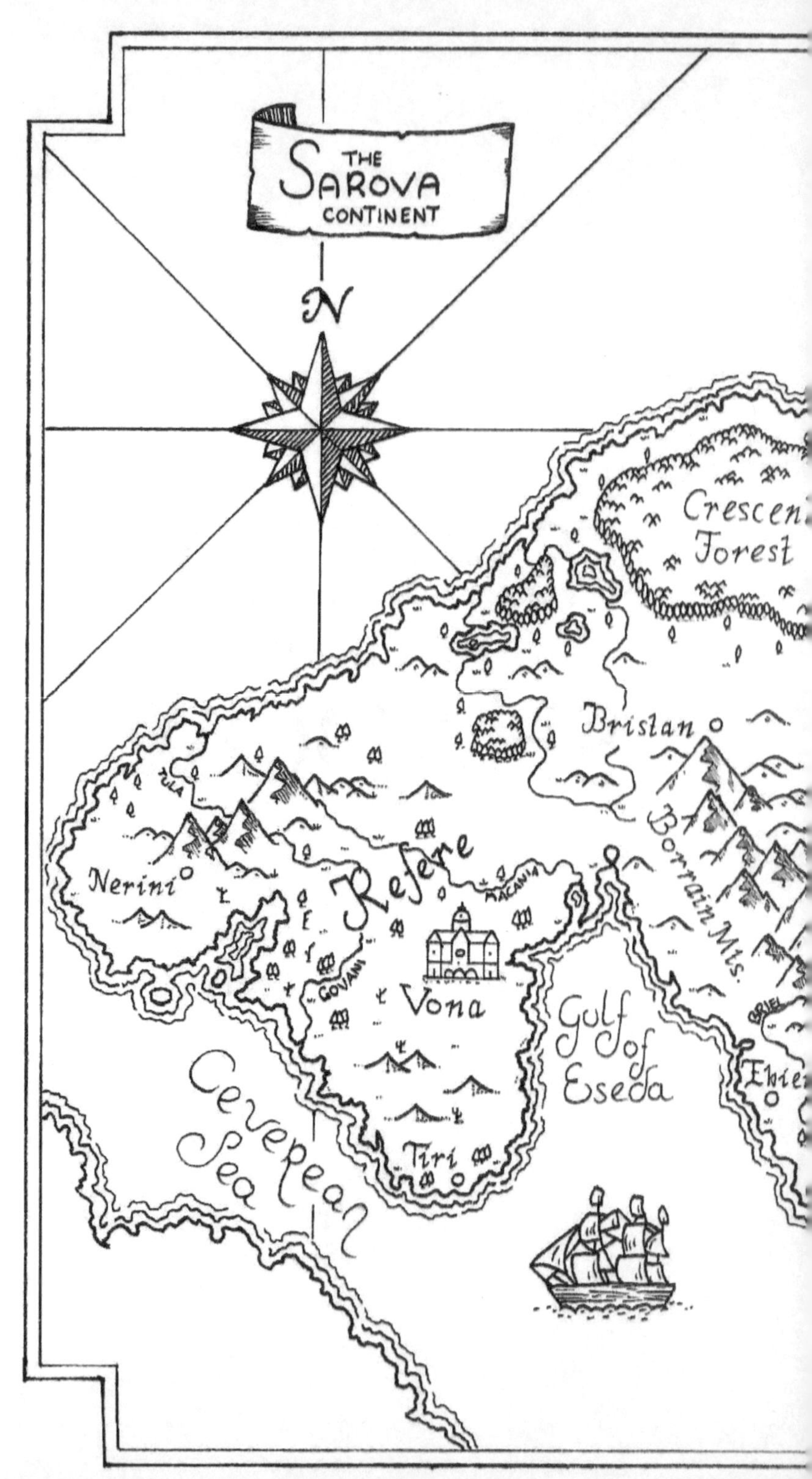

THE SAROVA CONTINENT
N
Crescent Forest
Brislan
Revere
Nerini
MACANIA
GOVANNI
Vona
Borrain Mts.
Gulf of Eseda
ORIEL
Ewien
Ceverel Sea
Tiri

Revnad
Nolnos Mns
Bulvarna
Isardra
Viritik Bay
THE DEEP
Luxler
Candul Region
Tandera
Mardon
RIST
BRIN
Kitsamo
itrel
Moshati
Okwa
Shi Lun
SERENDEN
RISTWACHI
Lahsi
rauselle
Risa Chanel
Virienne
Gevana
Isvedara
Santiel
e Coast
Amantian Ocean

For all my readers

~

To receive free stories, first dibs on ARCs and beta reads, and general all-around VIP treatment, sign up for my newsletter at vip.cfeblack.com/join.

We are born with the ability to see what others cannot: A light invisible to the world. To see this light is to live in shadow. To abuse this power is to pull the world into night. To use this light as it was intended brings oneself from darkness to day and brings about a dawn which no night can overcome. For this dawn we search. For this dawn we wait.

– from the *Canticle of Magic*, Volume I

Stepping out into the sunlit square decorated in harvest colors, Alyana Barron closed her eyes and for a brief moment relished the sight of a thousand invisible fireworks bombarding her senses. The swirling, burning light emitting from within every person, every animal, every tree and bush and stone swallowed her awareness in a sea of noxious beauty. In her moment of distraction, she stepped into a pile of cow droppings, the squelch bringing her, rudely, back to reality. With a flick of her finger, she dispersed the offensive pile in a whiff of smoke.

"Alyana," her mother chided. "I saw that. Be careful, child."

For a girl trying to hide her magic, festival days were both the most dangerous and the most exhausting. Despite this, Aly looked forward to the harvest festival all year.

Autumn wreaths and handmade banners colored the streets of Kitrel, but Aly paid them little mind, her senses occupied by the glittering energy within every person she passed. This light, if she lost her willpower, called to her magic like a carcass to a starving raven.

Decorative pumpkins lined the streets. Cattle adorned with

fall wildflowers plodded down the main road. Wagons of hay and barrels of fresh apples rolled behind the moving beasts. The village had gathered for the festival, as had a few families that lived outside the town, like Aly and her mother. Most of the faces Aly recognized, but not all. She was always glad to see new people; it meant Kitrel was worth visiting or, better yet, worth moving to.

And maybe it would bring in someone who might not hate her for being a sorcerer.

Aly breathed in the scents of the festival, a mixture of dry hay and sweet pumpkin bread wafting from the baker's open door just behind her. The sun shone in a bright blue sky, warming her pale skin against the autumn chill. Pausing by the road, Aly smiled and forgot to concentrate on suppressing her magic.

The energy in the world around her exploded in her consciousness. Her body tingled with the ocean of magic at her disposal. The rush of it was hard to ignore, harder to curb. Each cobblestone, each blade of grass, even the air carried power she could use—if she wanted to.

With her eyes closed, she sensed where the trees stood along the square and where the river flowed under the bridge that connected the two halves of the town. People burned like wildfires in her mind, their energy stronger than any plant or rock— and like wildfires, their brightness also swirled with clouds of smoky darkness. The draw of their energy, their *truth*, pulled on the magic inside her, like two small magnets turning toward one another.

After a moment, Aly opened her eyes, letting her mind become distracted once again by sights and sounds and smells. She knew better than to let herself feel that energy for long. To feel it was to *want* it, and Aly had promised her mother no more incidents. She glanced at the place where a very large tree had stood two years ago, the tree she'd accidentally set on fire during a harvest festival bonfire. She'd merely been trying to warm up, but magic was a beast, hard to tame.

Which is why, despite her mother's warnings, Aly had been practicing her magic relentlessly. She wouldn't mess up again.

It will bring the darkness to you, Aly's mother had warned. A keen fear flickered in her mother's eyes whenever Aly had performed magic around the house as a child. Aly had hated that fear in her mother's eyes, so she'd tried for years to quiet the need for magic that lived inside of her; but lately her ability to ignore the energy in the world around her was waning, as was her desire to do so.

Aly pulled just a little heat from the sunbaked grass beneath her and used it to warm her shivering mother. Renna sighed as her body stopped trembling, and Aly smiled. She didn't think Renna even knew Aly had used magic. She'd gotten subtler.

The few families of Kitrel greeted each other with hand-shakes and hugs, approaching each other so easily. Aly, who'd lived near Kitrel her whole life, was greeted by no one. A few townspeople smiled at her and her mother, but none spoke to them. The people of Kitrel had stopped whispering about the pale girl living with the dark woman, but that didn't mean they had accepted them. They were the strange, quiet pair who lived in the cabin down by the waterfall. The waterfall that, lately, was said to have healing powers.

Rumors often held some truth in them, but Aly was grateful the people of Kitrel hadn't figured out they had a sorcerer living in their midst—yet. Sixteen years ago, Renna had fled the presence of an evil magic in the north, a swaddled Aly tucked under her arm. Although magic had killed Aly's birthmother, caused her own father to disown her, and nearly killed Aly on the day she was born, Aly found it harder and harder to hate the power nestled in the world around her, power she alone had access to.

Despite the sermons coming out of the local abbey that spoke of magic as a gift from Theod, in Kitrel, sorcerers were spoken of with disdain, as that which only the high nobility, sequestered away in their fine homes, could afford. Magic was a dividing line, and the people of Kitrel were outside of the line.

Lady Ferra, Kitrel's only noblewoman, stood at the end of the lane, holding a parasol and looking disinterested at the happiness around her. As was the case with the rich, a cluster of people stood around her. Aly scanned the faces and hands of the men and women surrounding Lady Ferra, searching for a far-off look, the twitching of a finger, any sign that one of them might be conducting magic.

The Ferras kept a Comforter, but Aly had never once figured out which of their attendants was the sorcerer. Their Comforter was the only other sorcerer in the entire village, and the man's magic was as much a secret as Aly's, confined as it was behind closed doors or, more importantly, *to* select people. Certainly, the farmhands working the Ferra land did not enjoy the comfort of magic's cool breeze or the ease of boiling a pot with a single word.

Lady Ferra spun the parasol against her shoulder, a sign the lady was secretly enjoying herself. If she were truly bored, the parasol would be perfectly erect and unmoving, something Aly had deduced over a few years of silent observation of the lady. Though a keen observer, Aly had yet to spot the sorcerer. Whichever person it was, he or she had mastered the art of remaining perfectly still while directing a spell.

I will be a Comforter one day, Aly told herself, for the thousandth time. *I will find people who are not afraid of what I can do. I will get out of here. One day.*

Beside her, Aly's mother hummed faintly. Though Aly had lived with the woman for sixteen years, she still couldn't identify the fragmented tune Renna hummed every day.

"Looks like Danny had himself a good harvest this year," Renna said idly, eyeing a wagonload of pumpkins rolling by. A small boy ran beside the wagon, a long-haired dog trotting along with him. "I'd like a pumpkin. Go fetch us a pumpkin, if you would." Renna dug a coin out of her skirt pocket and handed it to Aly.

Thankful for the errand and her mother's trust to complete it, Aly hurried off to the place where she knew Danny would stop his wagon. As she walked after the cart, someone shouted at the boy to move away from the dog. The boy grabbed the dog, lifted the long coat at his haunches, and flashed the dog's brand at the angry man, who mumbled something about cutting the dog's fur. Aly skirted the small scene with a smile directed at the terrified boy. But within seconds, the boy was skipping along again, the man moving on about his business.

The people of Kitrel were careful to spy the brands on all the animals, whether horse or dog or cat or cow. Aly couldn't fully understand the people's fear of unbranded animals. Unlike the rest of Kitrel's inhabitants, she could simply close her eyes and *feel* the magic of the animal, no brand needed. But for those without the magical ability to sense energy signatures, a brand was the only way to distinguish a housecat from a shapeshifting Canyon lyth. Every animal Aly had ever seen, save the birds in the sky and the fish in the pond by her cabin, carried a brand to mark it safe—to prove it was not a beast of the Deep.

The main village lane was short and the miniature parade lasted only a few minutes. The wagons headed over the bridge, across the ravine that separated the two tiny halves of Kitrel, and into the small square.

Aly followed the pumpkin wagon onto the bridge, staring at the misty depths below. The ravine had always fascinated her. Such a sharp, narrow split in the earth, right through the center of her small town. The river below churned over the rocks. Of all the structures in Kitrel, the bridge was by far the most awe-inspiring. It even occasionally drew some tourists from Mardon and Frauselle.

Despite the beauty of the bridge, this gorge was the main

reason Kitrel never grew. Too many people feared canyons. *Windows to the Deep*, the people said, thinking every canyon had some similarity to the one near Bulvarna that held the Black River. Everyone in Kitrel called this one a *ravine*, careful not to use the word canyon.

A few people gathered in the square across the bridge, ready to be first in line to buy the fresh produce heading their way. The old wood-and-plaster homes and businesses surrounding the square boasted banners from upstairs windows. One banner depicted the very bridge Aly had just crossed, the most notable feature of Kitrel. Another banner boasted the symbol of Tandera, a phoenix rising toward heaven. A street performer juggled squash near the open door of the local pub.

Aly found a place to sit in the center, on the steps of a small obelisk. Danny's pumpkin wagon rolled to a stop over the cobblestones. The boy and the dog raced back toward the bridge, where several more wagons were crossing. Weather-worn fieldhands led the cows and oxen, their expressions both proud and tired. They had worked hard to provide the yield in the carts behind them.

Watching the carts rolling her way, Aly smiled at the celebration around her.

She suddenly felt something strange. At first she'd thought it was just the carts rumbling by, but as she held her hand against the stone obelisk, she realized the tremors rumbled under her feet. The stone pillar vibrated.

A girl sitting on the obelisk's steps looked up at Aly with wide eyes. "Do you feel that?"

Aly ignored the girl, immediately scanning the square, the bridge, the lane beyond for any signs of what could be causing the ground to shake. A few shouts sounded in the square. The cattle pulling one wagon ground to a halt, stopping the small parade.

Reaching out with her magic, Aly fully opened her mind to

everything around her. She sensed the bright energy in the girl beside her, the obelisk, the cobblestones, the distant river surging below the bridge.

Then Aly found the source of the tremors.

The stones below the bridge were moving. Pushed too long by the raging water, a fissure had opened up under the pilings beneath one of the bridge's main support arches. She could feel the water pushing into the crack, the cement beginning to give way.

The bridge, though it had held for two centuries, was breaking.

Her grip on the obelisk tightened in fear. On the bridge, the animals sensed their danger, but for some reason, they wouldn't move. They were frozen in terror.

One man, who was leaning out over the bridge's railing, turned and yelled, "The bridge! It's the bridge!" He ran with all the speed his legs could muster, abandoning the stalled carts and the petrified boy calling desperately for his dog, who was still trotting to the other side of the bridge.

A loud *snap* split the air and Aly's concentration. The noise and the flash of fear severed her mind from the sources of magic around her. Ahead, the bridge shook visibly. Screams rose all around.

And still the terrified animals would not move. The bricks began to shift.

The bridge was coming down.

Aly added her own scream to the frightened sounds all around. She opened her mind to the world's energy. There were at least a hundred witnesses and a dozen reasons Aly shouldn't use her magic.

But if Aly did nothing, people would die.

As the farmhands abandoned their hard-earned crops and their valuable animals to run for their lives, the easternmost arch cracked and the bricks shifted with a dreadful crumbling sound.

Within seconds, Aly had touched and rejected every source of energy around her. The pavement beneath her, the obelisk beside her, the air around her—all were too small to fuel the magic she needed to save the bridge.

The water. It'll have to be the water.

She had never pulled from something so far away before, but she had to try.

Gripping the obelisk for support, she closed her eyes and attempted to separate her mind from the screams, the tremors, the sounds of rocks breaking. She decided not to make herself invisible —to vanish now would be to draw more attention than necessary.

With all the concentration she could muster, she searched for the power of the river below. When she found it, it hit like a freight train.

Glad for the stone support beside her, Aly leaned against it and *pulled* on the energy flowing in the river. It rose to her silent command.

With that energy fueling her, she ordered the pieces of the bridge back into position. She demanded they hold together, fusing bricks and stones where they had cracked. She was barely aware of her surroundings and the change in the noises around her. Sweat formed on her temples and down her back. Her breathing intensified.

She kept pulling from the river, which still had more to give. In her mind, she nudged the animals forward, into the square, and resealed the cement holding the archway to the stone beneath it.

Before she opened her eyes, she searched for any fraction of light coming from water that might be between the piling and the rocks it stood on. When she found none, she hoped her actions were enough and opened her eyes.

The city around her was in chaos.

People were still shouting. Some were crying. Others were hugging. But they were all *smiling*. One pair of cows trotted down the road, the wagon full of wheat sacks bouncing slightly as the beasts fled.

The girl who had been sitting on the obelisk's base was gone. Aly stood alone in the center of the square. Ahead, the bridge still stood. No one was on it, but it looked whole.

A surprised half-laugh escaped from Aly's mouth. *I did it*, she thought, staring at her handiwork. *It actually worked.*

"A miracle!" shouted one woman.

"Kitrel has seen the hand of favor!"

"It was *magic*."

People clustered around the entrance to the bridge on both sides and along the balconies of the buildings that daringly jutted out over the narrow ravine. Aly shoved her hands in her skirt pockets and drifted toward the bridge to better hear what the people were saying. So far, no one had said a word about her.

Maybe no one saw me. Maybe they'd all been too focused on the bridge.

Among the small crowd gathered on the other side of the bridge, Aly spotted her mother's face. Renna scanned the crowd until she locked eyes with Aly. From that distance, Aly couldn't read her mother's expression.

No one seemed willing to cross. She understood why the others distrusted the bridge, but *someone* had to be the first across, and she knew better than anyone that the bridge would hold.

She pushed through the crowd and onto the bridge.

Gasps and protests erupted from the people around her. She ignored them and proceeded toward her mother.

By the time she'd made it halfway, several others had

followed her onto the bridge, the celebration bursting across the small space.

Good, they trust it. She knew the city would send men down to examine the pilings, but she hoped they wouldn't find any remaining damage. At least until the water won the constant war again.

Aly's presence on the bridge had drawn some attention, but the jubilee of the people quickly took over once again. They were all shouting about a miracle. With a few more steps, she was beside her mother.

Renna's eyes were filled with tears.

Uh oh.

She pulled her daughter into a hug. "You did well," Renna said against Aly's hair. "You couldn't very well let them die."

Relieved, Aly relaxed her shoulders and turned to listen to the people's response.

"You will *not* go calling this another of Kitrel's miracles," said a loud woman with blond hair. She stood with arms crossed. Her face was flushed.

Aly pushed closer.

The other woman, the baker's wife, dismissed her opponent with a wave of her hand. "I will! Just because you refuse to believe doesn't mean I can't celebrate the Maker's hand on our little town."

The first woman snorted. "Theod doesn't *do* miracles."

A few people clicked their tongues. More people gathered to hear this debate.

"How dare you!" said one man in the crowd, stepping toward the two women.

"I am not saying he isn't capable of them, but I am saying he doesn't do them. If you even knew what your own *Verad* said, you'd know he gifted *sorcerers* to do incredible things."

The man pointed at her. "You admit then that miracles come from Theod's hands!"

The woman uncrossed her arms and rolled her eyes. "They aren't miracles. They're *magic*...and not all magic is good. In fact, after what happened with the Canyon, I think *all* magic is corrupt. Why else did the sorcerers take to hiding the way they do? Masks and cloaks and all such nonsense."

A few nods from the crowd. Aly had heard of these *other* sorcerers, the Masters, employed by the rich as bodyguards. More powerful than Comforters, these elite sorcerers never revealed their true identity to anyone other than the family they served. She'd never seen one—not even the Ferras could afford one of these Protectors—and had never had the nerve to ask the local priest about them.

The man bristled. "The bridge was saved! That was clearly *good*. And how can you say magic is not good if it comes from the Maker?"

Aly was surprised the farmer was so devout. She'd seen these people in town, and some of them at worship services in the abbey, but she'd not known the truth or depth of their faith. She wasn't sure how true or deep her own went either, but she knew her magic had saved the bridge, and the lives of those on it. She had to believe the power inside her was good. She wasn't ready to consider what it would mean if her magic was bad.

Renna stepped up beside Aly, a look of rigid disappointment on her face as she stared at the small scene. Aly's shoulders curled in as she tried to become smaller.

The baker's wife picked up the farmer's line of reasoning. "Yes, Gwen, he's right. If you believe magic is behind these miracles, then you are outright admitting they are from Theod! How is that any different than what we've been saying all along?"

Gwen shook her head. "You people misunderstand. You don't listen! I said magic is corrupt *now*. Whether it always was, I can't say. We can't know if it's really from Theod or not— someone try to debate me on *that*, please! We simply can't know for sure. What we do know is that the magic that created the Canyon was evil. If you believe Theod is the source of magic, then you have to admit he's allowed it to do some pretty awful things. *Or,*" she paused for emphasis, turning to take in the crowd, "Theod never *wanted* magic in the first place and he's been trying to push it back all along."

The crowd was silent a moment. Aly's heart beat anxiously in her chest. *If magic is bad, then so am I.*

"Ay, ay!" said a few of the onlookers.

"That cannot be true," said a new voice. A man stepped into the small clearing where the debaters stood. He wore a surcoat, unbuttoned, and had on riding boots and gloves. He wasn't polished enough to look like nobility, but he carried himself too well to be common. Likely a merchant from Mardon. "Perhaps there is another explanation." He nodded politely to the woman named Gwen. "You admit, rightly, that not all magic is good."

The woman *humphed.*

"But that leaves the possibility that some is, in fact, good. Perhaps Theod has been fighting against the bad magic. Perhaps he left us the good magic so that we, too, could fight against it." A few people cheered.

Gwen glared at him. "We can't know any of this! You people just crave the miraculous. You want to think Theod is here, doing these things in our midst, but what if none of it is true? What if this so-called magic that saved the bridge came from our very own little canyon right here?"

The farmer shook his head. "No. Not every valley and river is evil. That's hogwash."

"You're saying just the *one* is? I find that harder to believe." Gwen lifted her chin.

"You can't deny that strange things happen here," the farmer continued. "The healings down by the waterfall. That storm a few years ago. The tree in the square that caught fire then just stopped burning suddenly. This bridge, today. You have to admit there is something special in Kitrel."

The man in the suit smiled. "Indeed, there is something special here. It's why I've come to visit." He scanned the faces of the crowd, and Aly darted her gaze away just as he reached her.

At that moment, another person burst into the small clearing where the argument was taking place. It was the girl who'd been sitting by Aly at the obelisk. She was breathless.

As all eyes turned to her, she lifted a hand. "She used magic! I saw it! It was *her*."

The girl pointed right at Aly.

2

Every face in the crowd stared at Aly.

The merchant took a step closer, and Renna's body stiffened beside Aly's.

Aly tried to keep her gaze down, but her eyes kept flickering back up to the man's face. His brown, wispy hair flowed in all directions. He had the start of a beard. He looked maybe mid-twenties, maybe younger. She was trying not to look at him.

"You are a sorcerer," he said plainly.

Biting her lip, Aly waited for her mother to speak. Aly couldn't lie, not without significantly weakening her magic for a time. She'd learned this both from a handful of sermons preached on the topic and from the way the world of burning light withdrew from her fingertips after she told a lie. She now took pains to always tell the truth.

"I'm sorry, sir, but we don't know what you're talking about," Renna said, her voice shaking as she spat out the lie. The woman, though not a sorcerer, was a terrible liar.

The man chuckled. "I see. You live in that cabin down the road, don't you? Place by the waterfall? I've heard of healings there. Yes, I'm quite familiar with these so-called miracles of

14

Kitrel. I think perhaps we know now the true source of those healings."

Neither Aly nor Renna replied. From the crisp pronunciation of his words, he was from the capital city, and men of the city who talked like that were usually too wealthy to come to Kitrel at all, but here he was.

"My name is Lord Weston Grey."

Aly bit her lip and dropped her gaze, hoping she hadn't offended this man by looking directly at him. *Nobility? Do the nobles in Mardon dress like that now?* People around her also fidgeted. Some offered small bows. One man extended to the lord a hasty welcome and a free night's stay at the only inn in town. Lord Grey lifted a hand and silenced the man.

"As it so happens," the man continued, "I am here to speak with this woman." He stepped closer to Aly and her mother. He bade everyone to attend to their own business and leave them.

A few people moved. Most didn't. They'd just witnessed magic and found out they had a sorcerer living among them. For small town folk, this was as bountiful as the harvest and would fuel their chatter well into the winter months. They wanted to hear what Grey had to say.

Aly glanced at her mother with an expression that she hoped said both *the secret's out* and *I'm sorry.*

Her mother nodded. "I know, dear."

Sometimes, Aly wondered if her mother really could hear what Aly was thinking.

"Come now," said Lord Grey, raising both hands in an exasperated manner. "Can't you people go away?"

Aly covered a small laugh. He clearly didn't know small town people very well. "Sir, follow me," she said, surprised at herself for uttering the order. She shrugged at her mother, who's mouth had fallen open, and walked toward the inn with its balcony that hung out over the ravine. She would find a bit of private space for them as she didn't feel it best to conduct magic out in the open. Besides, it would scare people if three adults disappeared from view.

Renna bustled along behind her, the woman's movements jerky due to chronic arthritis. Aly, pulling energy from the cobblestones, sent a small bit of magic into her mother's knees, hoping to lessen the stiffness and pain. Renna seemed to move a little easier, and Aly heard her sigh.

Lord Grey held the door to the inn for them.

"This way," Aly said, leading him to the balcony.

As she had hoped, the crowd stopped following them at the inn's entrance. But they would trickle in shortly to try to over-hear the trio's conversation.

Before they reached the doors to the balcony, Aly stopped. "You want to speak to us, and you don't want to be heard?"

Lord Grey nodded, eyebrows up.

"Then I'm going to make us all invisible. Okay?"

A smile curled across half of his mouth. "Perfect." Aly could have sworn he said *"You're perfect,"* but she dismissed that possibility because that made no sense.

Aly reached toward the energy of the fire burning in the inn's lobby, careful not to let herself be drawn too quickly or too forcefully toward its power, then dropped her shroud of invisibility around Renna, Lord Grey, and herself.

The three of them disappeared from the world.

"And they won't be able to hear us either." Aly pushed open the door to the balcony and slipped out onto the windy ledge. She quickly stole a little energy from the air and warmed herself.

When they were seated at a table, Lord Grey continued his explanation. "I had heard of the miracles in Kitrel. I'm a man of faith, but I know magic when I hear of it. Also, I happen to be looking for a sorcerer to train."

Aly's eyes widened. "Train?" Her mind drifted to the stories she'd read, a sorcerer trained to conjure spells that would keep a man safe in battle. *I'm no warrior.* She couldn't even imagine being on a battlefield with cannons and blood and rifles and more blood.

He stared at Renna as he spoke. "I am willing to train this young woman if she would be amenable to returning to Mardon with me."

Inside of her chest, Aly's heart flipped.

"What do you mean, 'train'?" asked Renna, her voice a bit harsh.

Aly gave her mother a pleading expression, but Renna never looked away from the man.

"I mean that her magic is something special." For the first time, he nodded at Aly. "Your actions today were extraordinary, even for sorcerers. Even this." He lifted a hand to wave at the three of them. "The fact that we're all invisible right now. *This* is powerful magic, and you don't even seem to realize how rare it is. What I seek is *talent,* and you have it." Aly blushed. "For one untrained, you are...impressive. I can train you to be better."

"Why?" Aly blurted, then snapped her mouth shut.

He smiled again, a slightly conspiratorial edge to it that made him suddenly more handsome. "Because magic like this shouldn't be left to your whims."

That wasn't what she'd expected.

"You don't know much about magic, do you? Your power, young lady, is special, even among those gifted like you. If you're *not* trained, then I might be hunting you later in life, rather than trying to recruit you to work with me." His arm rested casually on the table as he spoke of hunting her like an elk. "I'm in need of a sorcerer," he said plainly. "You do not know of me, I take it." Renna and Aly shook their heads. "I am on the king's council. I work closely with His Majesty, and I would like to hire you as my Protector." He tilted his head, as if to see whether Aly believed his words. "And, as part of that, I will train you to use magic in ways more powerful than anything you've ever known."

Aly's mouth fell open. "Sir?"

One hand slapped the iron table. On it was a ring with an enormous emerald in it.

Definitely nobility, she reasoned. *Maybe he's not lying.*

"Tell me, what has the most magic in it?" he asked her. Aly was silent, unsure how to respond. "Okay, between a rock, a tree, and a—" he glanced over the edge of the balcony, "—river, which has the most *fuel* for what you do?"

"The river, definitely. It's how I fixed the bridge." *Fuel, that's what I call it.*

The man shook his head, and for a moment Aly was afraid he'd correct her. "Like I said, impressive. That river down there is far away. Not many sorcerers could access it as a source while standing up here on the rim. And yes, the river has the most energy in it, compared to a rock and a tree, but you're wrong to think it's the best source."

"Sir, a rock has very little and a tree only slightly more. Do you mean fire is the best? I've often thought it's the best."

His eyes widened a moment. "No. No, fire is not the best. I caution you strongly *not* to use fire as a source. Fire, unlike other things you use to fuel magic, only gets stronger when you pull from it. It can quickly get out of hand that way."

Aly sank back in her seat. She switched her source for her shroud from the fire inside to the river below. She'd pulled from it to save the bridge, and maintaining a shroud needed much less magic than saving a crumbling bridge.

He leaned forward. "You said your name was Alyana Barron? Well, Miss Barron, I'm here to tell you that *people* are the best source."

"They are?" She leaned forward, matching his movement. "I've always felt their energy, but I've never been able to *use* it. Or at least, I've been too scared. I practiced on Mama some—"

she glanced at Renna, who frowned deeply "—but I stopped when I realized it might be hurting her."

His face was close enough now that Aly noticed his eyes were not exactly blue but green. Like hers. His stubble covered perfectly smooth skin. He was younger than she'd first thought.

"I can teach you how to use magic without hurting anyone."

She couldn't contain the smile on her face, but when she looked at her mother again, she cringed. "Mama, what is it?"

"Magic comes from *that place*. How can any magic be good?"

Grey leaned back. "Not all magic comes from the Canyon. In fact, most of it originally did not."

Renna shifted uncomfortably. "I know what the king's priests say, but I do not trust magic. It nearly killed my girl."

"But you trust your daughter?" Renna nodded. "Then how is that any different?" he asked. "You trust her, and the magic is *hers*. Mrs. Barron, it is the same thing."

"Not Mrs. Barron. Miss." She'd never married.

Grey's eyes widened a moment. "All right. Two Misses Barron. The elder Miss Barron, do you grant your daughter permission to come live at my estate and train to become a Master Sorcerer?"

Aly's heart quickened. It was all so sudden, but she knew more than anything that she wanted her mother to say *yes*. This was her chance to leave Kitrel. To master her magic. To move to Mardon and work for a man on the *king's council*. No battle-fields. No cannons. No blood.

This was her ticket out of obscurity. Out of the shadows. Out of the misery of solitude.

Renna looked out over the ravine. To Aly, it felt like an eternity before Renna turned back to them with her eyes still focused far away and her hair rustling around her face. She offered a faint nod. "She can't very well stay here now. The whole town knows what she is."

A small gasp of delight burst from Aly's lips. She cupped

both hands to her face, trying to contain the excitement building inside her.

"Very good," said Grey. "I'll send for her next week. We should have everything arranged by then." He stood, extended a hand to Renna, and shook firmly. "To the younger Miss Barron, I look forward to our endeavors. I believe you will be a sorcerer of great renown, when all is said and done."

"One thing, my lord," Renna said, drawing a sharp look from Aly. "I need to know you can keep her safe, protected from people who wish her ill." Renna's face darkened as she spoke, and Aly saw the same fear in her mother's eyes that had confined them to the solitary woods her entire life.

"Miss Barron, I assure you, your daughter will be safe. From what I can tell of her skill, she won't need me to protect her."

3

Aly peered wide-eyed out of the carriage. With trembling hands, she gripped the leather seat beneath her. Her thoughts were haywire—always a dangerous thing when magic was involved. As the carriage rumbled to a halt outside a massive, ivy-covered manor, her fingers pierced through the leather and into the cushion beneath.

"Oops," she muttered, snatching her hands into her lap and looking at the holes in the leather. She'd been thinking about what would happen if she left fingernail marks in the seats of Lord Grey's carriage. She had to be more careful and not let her mind perform magic inadvertently. The possibilities were too awful.

"I know you're nervous, honey," Renna said, eyeing the seat.

Aly took a deep breath and tried to calm her racing mind. Without a word, she sealed the leather back together, and when her eyes reopened, the holes were gone.

"Mama, I...what if I can't do it? What if I hurt—"

"Hush, child!" Renna grasped Aly's wrists and brought them across the small space into her own lap.

Aly leaned forward, her rich-lady's dress cutting into her

chest and thighs at the uncomfortable motion. At Renna's cabin, she'd only ever worn simple, country clothing. No bone-shaped torsos or necklines designed to draw the eye. The dress had arrived on their doorstep the day before she was scheduled to travel to Lord Weston Grey's estate. Surprisingly, it fit.

"I'm not ready for this," Aly confided, suddenly wishing she had more time to practice on Renna, more time to pour over the *Verad* at Kitrel's abbey and figure out things she'd missed before. *What will happen if I harm a man on the king's council?*

"You heard the man. You're special, Alyana," whispered Renna. "And to tell you the truth, I think you will be safer here. Now that word of your magic has spread in our town." Today was the official day of their parting, the day Aly would step away from what her mother could teach her and into the role she was born for: the role of a sorcerer.

A prickle of fear pinched the sides of Renna's eyes.

"You never wanted me to do this, to be *strong*," Aly muttered, her cheeks warm at the truth she was confessing.

"Oh, Aly," breathed Renna, a look of shock on her face. "I have always wanted you to be strong. But I know from experience that strength alone is not indicative of goodness. The magic of the Deep is strong, and it is evil. You will grow stronger here, but know that your strength comes not from what you move or change with your magic, but from who you are."

With a glance out the window, Aly's sorrow about leaving her mother was replaced with a fear of what she was stepping into. The air showed their breath, but Aly was sweating.

"Thanks, Mama."

Renna's life as a nurse in Bulvarna had shown her something truly terrible about magic, but Renna had never disclosed the details. Living that close to the Canyon must have been terrifying. She'd fled to Tandera, to a town far from the Canyon and far from the well-traveled roads between the big cities. She'd even chosen to live outside the small town of Kitrel, in the remote cabin where Aly had spent her entire life. The estate before her, situated at the edge of the capital city, represented a world Aly knew nothing about.

"We must consider that perhaps you were meant for this." Renna smiled softly, easing some of Aly's tension with her words. She glanced out the window as a man opened the carriage for them.

Meant for this. It was the most her mother had ever said in regard to Aly's magic being good. She always had the feeling Renna knew more about magic than she cared to explain, but Aly also recognized that her mother's knowledge was buried with a deep pain, and Aly had never wanted to probe that darkness with questions.

Aly accepted the butler's hand and descended from the carriage onto the fine gravel drive. Neatly trimmed bushes lined the front of the house.

"One man lives here, all alone?" she asked, staring up at the façade. A bright fall sky greeted her.

"Hardly alone, your ladyship," said the butler. "It takes some thirty staff to keep up the estate."

Aly blinked. Thirty? This guy had too much money.

Stepping forward, she nearly tripped on her dress. With a grunt, she grabbed the hem and marched toward the front doors. When she didn't hear her mother following, she turned and asked, "Mama, aren't you—?"

Her mother's face peeked out of the carriage. Her brown hair was mostly grey and her skin bore the look of hard winters, despite Aly's ability to keep their home warm even on the coldest of nights. This woman had dedicated her life to Aly, and now Aly was leaving her. With a small knot clogging her throat, Aly hurried back to the carriage.

"Mama, I will come visit. I *will.*"

Her mother pushed some loose brown hairs out of Aly's face.

"You needn't worry about me, my dear. I couldn't be more proud. Or more *glad* that you will be safe here."

"If he has *that* much money, he can't be as reclusive as we were led to believe. Rich people always have others around them." At least they did in the novels she'd read, and the Ferras' busy home supported this notion.

Renna grabbed Aly's head and kissed it. "He assured us you will not be known to the public or to the courts. Now go." She offered a small smile, but her eyes were rimmed with tears.

Aly obeyed, as always, and turned back toward the house of Lord Grey. They'd found out as much as they could about Grey in the week since their conversation on the balcony. As the youngest man on the king's council, he'd inherited a fortune when his father died from winterspell, the violent flu that claimed a handful of victims each year. A trained sorcerer could have healed the man, but Grey's father had not sought magic as a means of healing. Renna wasn't the only one who distrusted magic.

"Ah, here he is." The butler's voice interrupted Aly's thoughts.

Grey burst from the front door of the estate. His dark hair was not brushed and his waistcoat was unbuttoned. He bounded down the steps with a smile, not seeming like the stiff nobleman she'd met in Kitrel. Aly didn't find him terribly handsome, but she was surprised by how *normal* he looked for someone so rich and important.

"So glad you've made it." He stuck out a hand as if to shake Aly's.

She stared at it. She'd never shaken anyone's hand before. Touching people had inadvertently caused at least two disasters in her early years, when her magic was wilder.

His hand remained lifted toward her. "If you're worried that I'm afraid of you, I'm not. And if you're looking at my hand like that because you've actually never done this before, then we have more to learn than magic," he said, voice teasing, brow raised.

Aly shook his hand.

"Okay, we'll need to work on that." He frowned down at her hand and wiped away what was surely her sweat.

A blush flooded Aly's cheeks. *I could crush your hand into butter next time, if you'd prefer.* She thought about saying it, but figured since it was her first day on the job, she shouldn't anger her new employer. Instead, she followed him into his home's foyer, offering one last wave to Renna before the butler closed the door.

With the click of the door, Aly felt like her old life had been sealed away for good. Her heart hammered in her chest. Renna was gone, but rather than sadness, she felt both excitement and regret. Here she could learn the intricacies of magic that only the most elite sorcerers ever learned. Yet, by leaving Kitrel, she had left Renna to the whims of the seasons and the inevitability of age.

However, she fully intended to send Renna what money she could. Aly's stipend, as stated in the contract with Lord Grey, had made Renna's jaw drop. As long as Aly remained under Lord Grey's tutelage, serving as his Protector, she would receive a handsome sum.

The butler offered to take Aly's traveling cloak. He disappeared down a marble-tiled hallway, her cloak folded perfectly over his arm.

She stared at an enormous painting hanging across from the bottom of a wide, wooden staircase. The house smelled of wood and fall air. Aly noticed that many of the windows were open, letting in a chilly breeze. Aware of Grey watching her, she stood still, chin lifted, hands neatly clasped at her waist. She didn't want him to see the battle going on inside her.

Grey turned to observe the painting she still faced. "Do you like art?"

Aly didn't answer. Renna hadn't been able to afford art. Except for the few sloppy paintings Aly had created as a child and the many quilts Renna had made, their cabin had been devoid of decoration.

Grey stepped closer to the painting, allowing Aly a moment to stare at his back. He was fit, which seemed odd for a man who had enough money to never lift a finger. He was tanned from hours in the sun; also unusual. Lord and Lady Ferra, Aly's only real exposure to nobility—and country nobility at that—hardly ever spent time outside, and when they did, they hid from the sun beneath parasols or large hats. Grey's hands fidgeted and twitched behind his back, unable to remain perfectly still.

"My father commissioned this piece. He said he wanted a piece that depicted life and death, so that he could always be happy that he was alive." Grey glanced over his shoulder. "He commissioned it when a sorcerer nearly killed him."

Aly's face betrayed her shock.

He chuckled. "I didn't commission the thing. He did. I never moved it because it's too big, and I like how the artist captured the light on her face." He turned away from Aly and nodded up at the visage of a woman—the depiction of death—half-obscured by a shadow as she hovered over an oblivious man standing on the prow of a boat.

"Do you like it?" he asked, turning back around. He waited for an answer.

"No. Not now that I know what it means," Aly admitted, wanting to move on.

"No, forget that. Do you like the piece? I mean, do you like art? I have rather a good bit of it, and I thought if you enjoyed Yvesy, I could show you several more of his."

"Yvesy?"

The man shook his head, tossing his loose hair slightly. "You really don't know who he is, do you?" He ignored her annoyed expression and continued, "I see you've been living under a rock for what, sixteen years? Seventeen?"

"Sixteen."

"You admit you've been living under a rock?" He smiled.

"I don't think I have to admit anything. It's obvious."

He nodded, approving. "So it is. I suppose I see your mother's reasons. But I have to say, not knowing who Umberto Yvesy is? Such a shame. Have you ever heard a symphony?"

She stared at him.

His face wilted slightly, losing just a fraction of the joviality he'd held a moment ago. "Well, then. Much to learn, indeed. Come. We've got *Clarentine* in the Green Room, if you'd like to see it." He smiled broadly.

"Who is Clarentine?" *And why did he say she was an it?*

He blinked at her, then stepped off toward a drawing room with double doors that opened into the foyer. She followed. The Green Room was a formal sitting area complete with an ornate mantle and two small chandeliers. He pointed at a painting hanging at the back of the room, perfectly visible from the doorway. It was in a place of prominence, meant to catch the eye of all guests who entered.

Clarentine stared back at her.

Grey stopped a few paces behind her. Aly could feel his energy burning and didn't have to look behind her to know exactly where he stood.

"The painting, made famous by King Gevar's admission that it looked like his wife, Isabelle, spent years hanging in the museum in Mardon. I bought it after Father died. I figure, what better way to spend all this money than to buy art. The best art."

"Is Yvesy your favorite?" Aly asked, walking closer to the small painting. "How many do you have?"

"Yes, and three."

To have enough money to buy the world's most famous painting for your own drawing room. Must be nice.

She spun to face her new employer, unsure why they were discussing art. "Shall we begin?" She didn't want to wait any longer. Her nerves were killing her, and she wanted to get the first dose of Truthpulling out of the way.

If he was surprised at her forwardness, he hid it. He nodded and lifted a hand toward a velvet couch. "Please. I'll call for tea."

"No tea." Aly sat, back erect, hands in her lap.

"All right, no tea." Grey took a chair opposite her and crossed his legs. He looked relaxed, despite the fact that he was about to grant her permission to access the Truthwell inside him.

For a moment, he just stared at her, his head tilting back and forth every few seconds. His foot jiggled in the air.

Aly tentatively let her consciousness approach his bristling, pulsing energy. To her, it was like a type of light, almost tangible. She could sense patterns in it, but they moved too often, like a swarm of gnats. She'd only ever pulled truth from one other person—her mother—and that had not gone well. From that she had learned not to pull too hard or too quickly.

"Whenever you are ready," he said.

"I'm done."

He sat up quickly. "*What?*"

Aly pressed back against the couch, as if to shrink away from him. "I did it already, my lord."

"Weston, please, or Grey. Most people call me Grey. Tell me, what exactly did you *do?*" He leaned on his elbows. There was no anger in his expression, only curiosity. "I didn't feel a thing." Then he leaned back. "Wait, I do feel a bit warm. Is that you? Magic generally makes me feel cold."

Aly shook her head, then nodded. "Magic makes the air feel cold." He blinked at her attempt to correct him. "But I took a small bit of heat from you, yes."

"Then I should feel cold, right?" His voice held the hint of sarcasm and a touch of excitement.

"No. I did it fast enough that all you felt was your body replacing the lost heat. To you it would feel like you climbed a flight of stairs quickly, or something like that."

He slapped his hands on his knees. "No sorcerer is *that* good. You could be making the whole thing up to impress me."

Aly eyed him with a hard expression. "I do not lie, sir."

"Oh, I know." He waved a hand to dismiss her words. "All you magic folks never lie. How could I forget?" Definitely sarcasm now.

"We don't. It weakens our magic."

"Aly, I'm joking. I bet *you* don't lie. I just find it hard to believe you pulled energy from me without me knowing." He stood. "That's dangerous. That's...downright wrong."

"How is it wrong if you gave me permission?"

Grey tapped the back of his hand against his mouth, contemplating. "I don't know. Show me something else then. This house feels a bit chilly, don't you think?"

"Too rich to cut your own firewood?" she asked before thinking.

Weston Grey froze. She waited for his retaliation.

None came. "Warm the rooms, Alyana."

She nodded. "I'm assuming you want me to use you? There's enough stuff in here that I could warm the room without using you."

He cocked his head, then sat back down. "Yes, I want you to *use* me. Though we should clear one thing up: when you access the truth inside of me, you aren't *expending* it, like you do when you pull from a tree or a bird. Truth in a person is infinite."

Aly stared at him, then nodded slowly. "What about the river? It feels infinite. That's why the river fuels so much better than a rock or a plant."

"The truth in it is constantly replaced because it's flowing. It's not infinite. Unlike a tree or bird, it can't die when you use up its truth. Water *is* a good source, just not the best."

"So the truth inside a person can't be used up? I can't accidentally kill you, then?" she asked with a hopeful smile, but his frown exposed the strangeness of her words.

The lord watched her with intense eyes. "You can, in a sense, burn up so much at once that the person would die. To use that much, you have to have access to all of it to know exactly where it all is and how to use it in one single act. Few can accomplish that. Those who have, well, they knew what they were doing. They *wanted* to harm. But I don't think I have to worry about that with you, Alyana."

"Aly."

He nodded. "I'm here to let you learn the intricacies of Truthpulling. I'm giving you access to all the truth inside of me. It's an infinite Well, Aly. Even if you tried to pull it all at once, I doubt you'd ever scratch the surface. You can't hurt me by pulling more of it. I *want* you to try to use more. Every day. Every time we do this, I want you to try to find *more*."

"Find it, sir?"

Now he grinned. "You might be surprised to know that a person's truth is not all right there, hanging out at the surface; it is not easy to grab, the way it is in rocks and flowers. The Master Sorcerers take years to learn how to access all the truth inside of someone. Like I said, it's an infinite Well; that takes some time to plumb. And now I'd like you to warm the *entire* house."

How big was his house? She'd only ever warmed her tiny cabin in the woods. "I'm no Master. I have only practiced on my mother."

"I'm not afraid of you," he said again. He clasped his fingers and set them on his knee.

"Very well."

Aly closed her eyes, a little surprised by his trust in her. She could feel the Well of his energy and focused solely on that. She released all other thoughts, like birds from a coop. She'd practiced this many times over the years, so stillness came almost instantly. However, the precision necessary to tap into a human's energy was something she had rarely attempted. Take too little and the magic wouldn't work. Take too much and the person could die. He said it was difficult to kill someone this way, but she didn't want to risk it. He'd also said saving that bridge was impressive, but to her, it had been fairly easy.

She pulled the energy within him. It sparked against her own magic, flaring quickly and then resisting. This resistance was tricky, requiring more pull to overcome it, similar to what had happened with her mother. When she'd practiced on Renna, she'd pulled too hard the first time; her mother had fallen down, bruising her hip. After that, she'd pulled too softly a dozen times until she had finally succeeded in pulling enough energy to perform magic and catch her mother when she fell. For some reason, Renna always seemed to fall down when Aly used this kind of magic. After a few more tries, Aly had given up, not wanting to hurt her mother anymore.

Holding her breath, Aly gently tugged. The magic in Weston Grey relaxed, easing into her control. As soon as she had a firm mental grip on it, she commanded a steady yet small amount to raise the temperature in the room. When she felt the air temperature rise, she coaxed just a bit more energy out of him and imagined the whole house with comfortably warm rooms.

Grey's eyes widened. A loose, shocked smile pulled one side of his mouth. "Well, toss me," he cursed under his breath. "You really are good."

Aly looked down, her cheeks warm, not from the rising temperature, but from conducting magic. It always made her hot. Warming a place took even more energy than cooling it, considering magic stole heat from the places it passed. She expelled the chill caused by her magic out of the open windows. Aly had purposefully not commanded any additional heat into Grey's body, wanting him to feel her magic at work.

"If you warmed the house, Alyana, but froze me to do it, what good is that?"

"Aly. And I thought you *wanted* to feel me work?"

He chuckled slightly, then cleared his throat. "Indeed. But I'm freezing."

"Oh, sorry." She reached for the energy in the stone mantle, but thought better of it. She was here to master Truthpulling, and she had a man willing to train her. She pulled gently on the energy billowing within him, then directed heat into his body from the air. All this she did without a word, barely moving her fingers to conduct the simple spells.

Grey stared at her, his hands resting in his lap. She couldn't read his expression, and she quickly looked away, staring instead at the painting called *Clarentine*.

"You won't be here long."

"What?"

Her expression must have looked comically terrified, because he laughed loudly. "No," he said as he stood. "You'll be a Master before year's end. I have no doubt at all."

She blushed with a rush of excitement at his words. "A Master? Before the year *ends*?" That was in three months. She'd expected to train for years. "What does that have to do with me leaving?"

Grey paused at the doorway. "You'll find out." He flashed her a smile. "My guess is, in about three months."

4

Days passed before Grey summoned Aly to the drawing room. She'd begun to wonder exactly how much he needed her; more importantly, she wondered when she would be able to practice.

She was eager to perfect her magic, despite the dangers it posed. Every day without training was a day she felt vulnerable, a day that she would not be ready to protect Grey if called to do so.

Near the end of the week, when a bell rang in her room just after dawn, she knew she was needed. She dressed quickly, throwing on one of the simple dresses she'd brought from home. He hadn't told her where to meet, but she assumed it was the same room where they had practiced that first day.

The door stood open. He sat in the same high-back chair reading a newspaper. She conjured her shroud, making herself invisible and completely silent, and crept into the room. She hoped it might remind him what she was capable of. But when she removed her shroud, suddenly appearing on the couch across from him, he no more than blinked.

"Good morning," he said and folded his newspaper. "Quite the entrance." He nodded to her.

She couldn't tell if he was annoyed or pleased. She didn't like that.

His hair was even messier this morning, as if he'd had no time—or had taken none—to brush it since waking. He wore the same suit, with a waistcoat unbuttoned. He sat with his legs crossed, his foot bouncing slightly in the air.

"Would you prefer if I knocked?" she asked.

"Having a powerful sorcerer around is unsettling enough. I'd prefer if you didn't also drop out of existence to sneak around wherever and whenever you please."

The harshness in his tone startled her. "Sir, I wasn't planning to—"

"Just 'yes' will do."

She blinked. "Yes, sir." Glancing at her hands, she said, "I thought you weren't afraid of me."

"Oh, I'm not. But this is *my* house, and I have a way of running it that I intend not to alter. You will remain visible here, Aly. Always. Unless I specifically ask you to hide yourself."

Something about his tone suggested he was nervous, as if there was something in his house he didn't want her to find. This, of course, only made her more curious to explore. He didn't tell her *not* to look around, just not to do so while invisible. "I will honor your request," she said aloud, so that she'd have to obey it. If she didn't, then her words would be a lie, and her magic might weaken as a result. She hadn't tested the waters on *future* lies yet, but she didn't want to test them today.

He nodded, satisfied.

"Sir, I know you called me here, but can I ask a question?" She had so much to learn, and she wanted to discover it all immediately. The urge to *know* was almost overwhelming. "Why do lies weaken magic?"

Grey pursed his lips and remained silent for a moment. "I

believe that's a question for someone more knowledgeable than I." Aly's heart sank. "You aren't very good at keeping a straight face, are you?" He chuckled. "I think I know someone who can answer all your questions."

"I'd hoped *you* could."

"I'm sorry to disappoint you."

She stared at him. No sarcasm or jest shone out of his eyes or in his small smile. She studied every bit of his face, careful to try to learn his tells and his mannerisms. Opposite of what he'd said about her, from what she'd seen of him, he tended to keep a fairly consistent facial expression: this thin-lipped smile. It was there when he was firm, and it was there when he was poking fun. It was completely relaxed and thus utterly perplexing.

"You look confused," he said after a moment. He held his fingers steepled in his lap.

Why is he so good at reading me? I hardly know him. "Sorry."

"You don't always have to apologize for everything."

"Sor—right. Why did you call me?"

He slapped his hands on his knees, stood, and paced over to the fireplace. "I would like you to start a fire here." He rubbed a hand on his neck, craning his chin up and around in a circle.

"Easy enough." Aly had created fires at home many times, but she'd used other sources of magic, not a person. She stood, too, just to take a good look at the hearth and the logs lying there. She lifted a hand toward Grey. This would require a little more precision to direct this magic, and it always helped to use her hands, if only to focus her mind on where the magic should go.

His eyes followed her hand. One of his own reached up to grip the mantle.

"Are you uncomfortable? Sir?"

Grey swallowed. "I think you should know something." He stared at her hand as he spoke. "Something that might help you understand why I never hired another sorcerer until now. It might help you understand why the energy inside me resists you." She was shocked he knew this, but she didn't interrupt. "My father." He swallowed again. "He didn't particularly like the way it felt for sorcerers to access the truth inside him, so he sent his children instead. He sent his children to be the fuel for his Protector."

Aly's eyes widened. Based on his tense posture during this strange revelation, whatever that sorcerer had done had not been pleasant. She'd never imagined a man would use his children as a source of power.

She burned with questions but wondered if they would sound rude. *How had the sorcerer Truthpulled if you hadn't given him permission? And how were you always there when the sorcerer needed you? And why? And what sort of magic was this sorcerer conjuring for your father? Why didn't your father like to be a source?*

She left all the questions unspoken.

"I'm sorry," she said. "Why do you let me do it?"

He glanced up at her. "Because you're not him. And because I love my country."

She wasn't sure what the last part had to do with their conversation, but she didn't want to offend him by questioning his motives, not when he'd just admitted he'd been abused by his own father. He was now revisiting the shades of his abuse by letting her access his truth.

"To light a fire on logs that dry and perfectly laid, you won't feel a thing." She hoped this encouraged him.

Instead, he frowned. "It scares me that I can't feel it. I could always feel it. Before." He looked at his hand, clicking his fingernails. Aly chewed her lip. "But I suppose my father's sorcerer was pretty awful, considering he nearly killed my old man and yanked on us so roughly it gave me breathing problems as a child."

She bit her lip so hard she flinched. "Us?"

"My sisters and I."

"Where are your sisters?"

He dropped his hand. "They live in town. They prefer to be right in the action." He hissed the words, as if he hated the thought. "My mother wants nothing more than for them to marry well. It's really rather a chore to be around them, and someone's got to look after this place."

"Of course." She had no idea what else to say.

He gestured at the fireplace. "Well, are we starting a fire or aren't we? If you'd prefer a challenge, Miss Barron, I'm sure I can think of something."

He wasn't handsome and was too old, but at that moment, Aly was struck by his mischievous smile. She hoped he didn't notice the blush on her face.

Before she answered, she lifted her hand again and within seconds had a fire crackling in the hearth.

"It can't be that easy," he said, staring at her, not the flames.

To avoid his comment, she said, "Sure, I'll take a challenge." She remembered, just barely, to add, "Sir."

"Good answer. Come with me."

They walked out the back of the house through the gardens overlooking a sloping field with a few horses grazing.

"I've never seen one person own so much space. The Ferras had land, tons of it, but it was all farmland. This…is beautiful."

He looked over at her. Despite barely knowing him, she felt comfortable as she walked beside him. His presence had a way of easing her nerves and making her smile. "You haven't seen the royal gardens, have you?" It wasn't really a question. "That'll change soon."

"The palace?"

He laughed when he noticed her face. "Yes, Alyana, the palace!" He waved his arms in a grand gesture, carefree and affable. "I did tell you I'm on the king's council, didn't I? We'll be going there for a state dinner next week."

She stopped walking. *The palace?* She'd only just left her rural life a week ago. She didn't know how to shake hands, and her clothes were peasant's garb. She'd never heard a symphony or seen a Yvesy until this man had shown her one. Now she'd be entering the royal palace. Very strange, considering he'd told them he was a recluse.

"Will I meet the king and queen?" She stood rooted to the spot, too awestruck to move.

Grey turned around, his hands in his pockets. He opened his mouth, but then closed it. Finally, he said, "Eventually, yes, but probably not this time."

Aly jumped with excitement and then fell back into line beside him.

She would get to *meet* the king and queen. Even in Kitrel, she'd heard stories of the queen. Queen Isabelle, who was really just a princess or something, but everyone in Kitrel called her the queen. She'd once been just Isabelle Carrington, nothing more than a commoner; a wealthy one, true, but still she had no title, no status, nothing but the most beautiful face the king had ever seen. He'd quickly been smitten. Her rise to the status of royalty had been the inspiration for a few modern folktales and the fodder of many girls' dreams.

As they descended the slope toward the stables, he said, "One of the things I'd like you to practice today is your shroud. In Kitrel, you demonstrated that you can cover more than one person. I guess I shouldn't be surprised." He lifted a hand toward her. "You're good at everything, apparently, but I want you to practice turning me invisible when I'm not near you, and maybe even while I'm riding a horse."

Not nearby? I didn't think that was possible. Aly didn't question this out loud. If this man said it was possible, she believed it, and would find a way to do it.

Moments later, she followed him into the large breezeway of an immaculate stable. A few stalls were filled with sleeping horses, but most of them had been turned out to pasture.

Grey walked up to one stall and slid the door open. The familiar scent of livestock comforted Aly, whisking her back to the streets of Kitrel and the harvest celebration that had so abruptly launched her into this new world. She would never be that girl again, the one afraid to do magic.

Here she was supposed to do magic. He'd told her to try to find *more* every day. A smile spread across her face as she contemplated what could be possible when she reached the level of Master.

"Like horses?" asked Grey, eying her from inside the stall. He stroked a red mare with one hand.

Aly snapped out of her musings and shrugged. She didn't love horses, but she thought they were pretty.

"Ruby here has had a bit of a long night, but I think that might make her less eager to bolt if she spooks while we're practicing. Eh, girl?" He patted her neck and then leaned in to give her a quick hug. "Come on, let's go."

He led Ruby out into the small paddock behind the barn. "First, let's just practice shrouding me and you." He looped the lead around a fence post. "If you're going to be good at protecting me, I need to know you can make me disappear. Not like you did in Kitrel, but from anywhere, from a distance."

Aly nodded. In her skirt pockets, her hands knotted around fabric. She had never before attempted to extend her shroud a distance, she'd only ever used it to hide herself, and occasionally Renna. She hadn't ever really known *how* she created the shroud, just that her desire to be invisible and silent had given her the ability to make it happen. Magic obeyed her thoughts; it was that simple and that profound.

Grey walked to the other end of the paddock. "Let's try from here. I'm not sure how distance affects magic. What do you know of it?"

She blushed and shook her head. "Not much."

"Don't lie, Aly." He grinned. "You patched that bridge and it wasn't that close to you."

Her cheeks flushed hotter. "The river was a strong source, though. It was far away, but it had a lot to give."

"Or maybe you're just strong."

She looked over at Ruby, avoiding his gaze.

"I've got more than that river, Aly. Let's see what you can do with it. Make me invisible."

For the span of a few seconds, she cleared her mind. She shut down all distractions and focused on the power she felt burning in Grey's body. The power was so vibrant, so deep, and so rich that Aly wanted to wade into it and lose herself, or snatch it all in an instant and be consumed by its power.

For a moment, she feared she would.

She opened her eyes, breathing quickly. The sight of Grey standing there reminded her of her task and dampened the urgency of the burning temptation to strip all the truth from him. *What in the world?* She had never felt so greedy when Truthpulling from a bush or a brook. She took in the horse beside her, the beautiful stable, the inviting fields, the green eyes of her tutor. Distractions made the temptation less overpowering, but it also made magic less precise.

Focus, she told herself. She closed her eyes again, but the energy coming from Grey was like the warmth of the sun and she was a frozen blade of grass, desperate for the light.

Suddenly, she surged her magic toward Grey's energy. She pulled on it, hard. It swirled into and around her magic. It flared, grew brighter, and then blinked out with a thud.

When she opened her eyes, she was sitting awkwardly on the ground, her legs splayed out before her, hands in the dirt.

Grey rolled to his side on the ground, right beside her. "What was *that*?"

"Did you push me?"

He sat up and ran a hand through his messy hair. "Aly, you… what happened?"

She stared at her skirt, which was now powdered with splotches of dirt, but so were his crisp, dark pants. "I don't know." *That's not true.* She knew, but she couldn't admit it.

Grey stared at her—she could sense his eyes on her. "That felt like…it felt like it did with *him*."

"Did it hurt?" Aly cringed before he even answered, afraid of the truth.

"No." Grey stood and held out a hand to her, pulling her out of the dirt. "No, I'm fine. But you. I was watching you. You sort of went all strange on me. Your eyes and your hands. Then I was right beside you, without even taking one step. Aly, you *moved* me."

She blinked before shaking her head. "I have never moved a person."

"What *happened*, Alyana? I need to know."

He was right. Truth was imperative in this scenario. She wanted him to know her weaknesses, her mistakes. After all, it was his life on the line, not hers.

"Actually, sir, there is something." She inhaled and looked at the fence, not wanting to watch his face as she explained this part. "When I feel your magic, or rather when I sense the energy inside of you, I…there's a moment when it's hard to—resist. It's like there's a part of me that wants to grab it all up at once." Shame reddened her cheeks. "I didn't do such a great job resisting it that time. I'm sorry."

Grey stroked his chin a moment. "I think you're wrong."

"What?"

"You didn't hurt me, Aly. You didn't grab all the energy inside me. I'm still here, aren't I? Remember what I said? You have to know where the energy is in order to use it. You *can't* kill me yet, Aly. You don't know enough about magic."

"That's comforting," she mumbled, crossing her arms.

"You are strong." He bent down to capture her gaze. "But I'm not afraid of what you can do to me."

"Maybe you should be."

"When we visit the palace, I will introduce you to Arthur Ondorian. He can set you straight about some of your worries." He placed a hand on her shoulder. Instead of feeling utterly out of place, it helped to calm her. "Your magic is a gift from Theod. Don't fear it. Trust it, and trust *me*. I promise, it'll be much easier that way." His hand fell. "I told you to search out the depths. Maybe what you feel is not a desire to steal all my truth but to discover it."

She blinked again. His face was nearly level with hers. He wasn't tall and commanding. He didn't even seem that old to her in that moment, but he did seem wise and entirely too trusting of a novice sorcerer he'd only just met.

"This time, do what I ask and make me disappear. You can do it, but I'll hold out my hands, just in case." He smirked.

Her cheeks blushed darker. She'd knocked herself down by pulling Grey across the paddock toward her. She'd smacked his body into hers. *Idiot.*

As he walked away, she couldn't even look at him. How could she perform magic without any thought or intention? It didn't work that way. Magic was intentional, if nothing else. It only ever acted as she *wanted*, even if her desires were unspoken, even unadmitted.

A sudden, embarrassing thought hit her and she cupped her hands over her face. Her magic *had* obeyed what she'd wanted. In a moment of unwelcome distraction, her magic had pulled Grey toward her. She didn't even like him, but he was the only man she'd ever really spoken to.

She was hopeless.

Maker above, don't let him figure that out, Aly prayed, rubbing her hands down her face in an attempt to wipe the mortification off her cheeks. Grey, however, was still walking toward his horse.

"On second thought, let me ride to the end of that field. You said you wanted a challenge."

5

The carriage rolled toward the royal palace on a moon-filled night. Aly's dress was even more elaborate than the one she'd worn the day she'd arrived at Grey's estate. She couldn't stop fidgeting with her hands and glancing out the window, as if it might offer her a quick escape.

"Good thing you'll be invisible tonight," Grey taunted, smirking at her wringing fingers.

She rubbed her hands along her hips, searching for pockets that weren't there. "I wish this thing had pockets."

After a week of practice, she could shroud Grey from a stone's throw away, but no farther. She felt inept as the days had proceeded with little improvement in her magic. She'd been so confident at first, fueled by his compliments, but her initial success had worn off. She was now struggling to accomplish what Grey asked of her.

Grey chuckled. "I assure you, that dress is far superior to those *things* you brought with you."

She frowned out the window, watching the grand city of Mardon roll by. She'd never seen the capital city before. Never seen famous art. Never been to a symphony. Never seen the king and queen. Never worn fancy dresses.

Will I ever fit in here? In this life? Attending dinners hosted by the king.

"Hey, you'll be fine," Grey added. His typical smile was still there, but it was perhaps a little warmer. Ever since that humiliating moment in the paddock, she'd avoided looking directly at him while conjuring. In fact, she avoided looking directly at him in general. She found reasons to glance around, to look at her hands, to feign interest in some piece of furniture or art in his house or, in this case, the stone buildings lining the cobblestone road.

"You won't need to create much magic tonight. Just go, watch, and enjoy."

"But not participate."

Grey exhaled. "We both agreed it's best if you remain invisible tonight. Sorry, Aly, but if I show up with a woman, talk will explode. No amount of magic can keep the gossipers quiet once they become wound up. You said yourself that you aren't ready for state dinners with royalty." He glanced at her hands again. "And to be honest, you'd stand out like a bee in a butterfly house."

"Thanks."

"You know it's true." He glanced out the window. "It's not the way you look. It's the way you act."

She wasn't sure what to make of that comment.

"Keep getting better at magic," he continued, "and I promise you'll get to meet the king. He'll *want* to meet you once you reach Mastery. He meets all the Master Sorcerers in his kingdom. At least, he tries to. He likes to know them personally, should he ever need to call on them."

"Smart man."

"He is."

They rumbled over the cobbled roads. Aly was so nervous

that she didn't even need to warm herself, despite the chilly evening. Grey wore a wool suit, his shoes shinier than the wet stones outside. He looked every bit the wealthy nobleman. Aly's dress fit her a little too well. Grey had insisted she have her measurements taken. That morning, a silver dress had been laid out on the couch in her room. She lacked much for the neckline to accentuate, for which she was grateful. She couldn't imagine sitting in this small space, Grey facing her, if her dress had revealed more than it already did. Fortunately, he never seemed to look at her like he cared about her neckline; she wasn't sure how she could perform magic with him if he had.

Though she would spend the evening invisible to the world, Grey had insisted she dress for the occasion. She needed to become used to the clothes, the way she would move in them. Also, if for any reason she dropped her shroud, she wouldn't be wearing her tattered Kitrel clothes in the royal palace. Though she felt uncomfortable, she couldn't help but love the way the dress looked. She felt important, something she'd never felt before.

"Here we are," Grey said.

They passed through a set of wide, elaborate gates, and Aly craned her neck around to take in the palace.

"Here," Grey said, laughing. He leaned forward, grabbed her shoulders, and traded places with her in the carriage. "Now, look."

She smiled broadly, pulled her shroud over herself, and stuck her head out the window.

The courtyard was lit with endless flickering street lamps that led her eye toward a brilliant façade. Pale stones rose in a grand fashion, dotted with a thousand windows. The corner towers rose into small points, and lights from below cast the royal palace in bright contrast to the night.

She was going to have dinner in the *palace*. Her entire life, she'd never dreamed of this.

Well, *she* wouldn't actually be able to sit and eat, as she'd be invisible, but she would still be present. She hadn't really figured out what she would do while Grey dined, but that didn't really matter as she stared out at the palace of the king.

Now that she was working with Lord Weston Grey, the royal palace would become part of her routine.

The girl from Kitrel, the secret sorcerer who'd spent her life hiding her abilities, had been replaced with someone new. Someone she wasn't really certain of yet. Not quite a Master Sorcerer. Not exactly invited to the palace on her own. Still not able to do magic out in the open, but no longer the girl living in the woods, afraid to do magic, afraid *of* magic.

The carriage stopped. She would one day learn to move the thing on her own, but they hadn't practiced this yet, and Aly couldn't conceive of pulling that much magic for such an extended time. Outside the carriage, Grey lifted his arm toward her, as if to lead her into the party.

"You can't see me, right?" She was certain her shroud was covering her. She let him hear her, then covered her sound once again.

"No, but I don't need to see you to know you're over there shaking like a wet cat. You can hold my arm if that will help. No one will know it."

She stared at him. Then, with a timid hand, she reached for his arm. "Can you feel that?"

He nodded. "Looks like your shroud doesn't hide your touch. Maybe we can practice that one day."

His words somehow made her uncomfortable. To practice that, they'd have to touch again. He could probably feel the tension in her fingers. She tried to relax, to feel at ease holding onto him. Instead, as he stepped forward, she gripped his arm so tightly that he let out a small chuckle. Her heart beat madly.

The fact that people couldn't see her soothed her nerves a little. No one would be criticizing her posture, her clothes, her lack of experience at court. She could observe without being observed. As she ogled all the dresses and jewelry of the other women in the courtyard, she was grateful they couldn't see her.

The grand foyer made Aly's jaw drop. Marble stretched in all directions. The high windows showcased the starlight outside. Light seemed to come from everywhere: wall sconces, grand chandeliers, even candles in tall candelabras along the carpet they walked.

She'd never seen anything so marvelous. She could make a candle burn with magic. She could light a fire. She assumed that she could fuel a chandelier, but she'd never tried.

Is all this lit with magic? Surely a king could find sorcerers to light his world, but would he?

A brief thought occurred to her that chilled her very insides. She wondered if there could be a whole group of people, caged somewhere in the palace, serving as energy sources for Masters who filled this place with light and warmth.

"Pretty, isn't it?" Grey asked casually as they filed in behind a line of guests.

She was surprised he had spoken to her, but she heard a voice behind her say, "Positively lovely!" Aly glanced back at the woman, who was busy staring up at the ornate ceiling. Of course, Aly wasn't really there. She wanted to ask Grey about the light, about the magic here, but unlike him, she couldn't speak aloud tonight. It was the frustrating side of being invisible.

She shook that thought from her mind and proceeded into the party at Grey's side, careful to avoid bumping into anyone.

They entered the grand ballroom, where two long tables were set with countless pieces of crystal. Towers of greenery and blooms rose at intervals down the tables. Pools of light burned from within each guest like a hundred tiny fires, each Truthwell calling out to Aly to be searched, touched, consumed.

She dimmed her mind to the energy around her, focusing instead on the grandeur of the ballroom.

The ceiling contained a mixture of golden woodwork and idyllic paintings of angelic beings. They wore flowing white robes, and their hands had a faint glow around them. However, Aly could not make out a single face, not just because they were so high above but because their faces were obscured by painted shadows.

She opened her mouth to point this out to Grey, then caught herself. Not only was she to remain silent, but surely Grey had been here many times and seen the paintings. She added this to her mental list of questions to ask him later. He knew about art, and she imagined he'd be able to explain the symbolism behind the figures' hidden faces.

Violins hummed in the corner, accompanied by a harp. The smell of flowers mingled with the powerful scents of perfumes and colognes. Aly closed her eyes and briefly relished the sensation of energy around her. A quick survey of the room revealed bright and throbbing Truthwells as well as dim ones—some so dark they appeared as smoke-like clouds concealing faintly glowing embers. With ease, she pinpointed Grey's energy signature as she'd memorized the pattern of the light inside him.

She was not using him to keep up her shroud tonight. She was simply pulling from the air around her. It created a slightly cool cloud, but she assumed Grey only welcomed this now that they were inside the ballroom, where the air was much warmer than it was outside. Likely, no one else would be aware of it as it only extended a few inches around Aly.

A man brushed past Aly, bumping into her shoulder and shoving her against Grey.

"Apologies, Lord Grey," said the man, who clearly thought he'd bumped into Grey. He pinched his brow, as if confused how he hit someone, then proceeded on toward a pair of chatting gentlemen.

Grey tucked his arm against his body, more securely pressing Aly's fingers into his rib cage. She moved closer, glad to have an anchor in this alien crowd. She'd never felt so out of place, so unprepared for the opulence around her. She fully agreed that invisibility had been the right choice.

A voice announced the guests should take their seats. Grey directed them toward the head of the table on the left, which Aly realized was actually to the right of a small table that sat perpendicular to the two long ones. It held five chairs, one for the king and queen, and three for their children. Aly had heard of the prince and princesses. Even in Kitrel, people seemed to have little else to fantasize about than the royal children's futures. Their sons could marry the princesses, and their daughters could marry the prince. Since the legendary wedding of Gevar and Isabelle, every family in the country thought their child would be the next commoner to marry into the royal bloodline.

The guests filed into their seats. Suddenly, Aly realized she would be released and left on her own. What was she supposed to do while the rest of the people ate? Were there any other sorcerers here?

As if just noticing a spider on her hand, Aly jumped a little as her eyes settled on a large figure in a white, broad-shouldered cloak. The person wore an elaborate mask with red and blue feathers that extended upward and a beak that covered half the face. This was a Master Sorcerer. Quickly, she spotted two others. A dark, beaded bear's mask concealed one sorcerer's face, and a shining golden lion's mask, complete with flowing mane, concealed another's. All three wore the white robe, hood up. Though visible, these people were as hidden as she was.

"Those are the Protectors, aren't they?" she hissed at Grey, close to his ear.

Aly had never met another person capable of magic.

She knew there was at least *one* other present as well. The

Royal Sorcerer. Though he or she was part myth, part history, even the people in Kitrel had accepted that the King of Tandera kept a sorcerer. All kings kept a secret sorcerer, the stories said. Grey had confirmed this.

He didn't even look up, but waited as a man pulled out his chair. "Yes."

In a wave of excitement, she dug her fingers into his arm and he let out a small wince. *Oops.*

She focused on a cloaked, masked figure. A sorcerer. She closed her eyes again and tried to find the sorcerer's Truthwell. Instead, she found nothing.

Odd, she thought. *Can a sorcerer shroud their Truthwell?*

She was wondering how long she would have to wait to ask her questions when Grey whispered, "I'll take my seat now. You ready?"

No, she thought, but remained silent.

"I highly recommend you visit the solarium. The library is fantastic, too." He was encouraging her to *explore* the palace. While invisible. "But don't go snooping."

She squeezed his arm, gentler this time, to say she understood. The thrill of walking through the royal palace at her leisure made her forget her hunger and that she wasn't invited to dine.

He lifted his elbow, signaling her to let go. "Don't worry," he muttered. "You won't go hungry tonight." He covered a fake cough and nodded to a man seated in the chair next to his.

She released his arm and stepped toward the wall. As Grey took his seat, she turned to the open ballroom doors.

It was time to disappear.

The palace was larger inside than it had appeared outside. After an hour of wandering, she still hadn't found the library or the solarium. She'd walked the grand stairwell from the foyer to the upper floors. She'd strolled down hallways full of art and gilded trim. The hallways became narrower and the decoration less impressive the higher she climbed and the farther she walked.

When the hallway abruptly ended at a locked door, she decided to turn around, but she had absolutely no idea how to return to the ballroom. A few turns and another staircase emptied her into a tall room hung with dozens of antlers and the heads of long-dead deer, moose, and elk. A stuffed tiger lurked in one corner. In another corner, near an enormous hearth, stood an animal on its hind legs; its face had been captured in a menacing snarl.

Aly started. It looked about to leap out at her. She forced a chuckle and stepped closer. *What are you?*

She'd never seen an animal like it. It resembled a large fox, was red, and had black paws, but it also had a bit of a mane on the top of its neck. Its teeth were enormous, and the look in its dead eyes was one of utter rage.

"You have never seen a foxblood, I take it?"

Aly yelped loudly, which echoed down the nearby hall. As she spun around, a bald man approached. He wore a suit, but was free of ornament. Unlike Grey's suit and the suits she'd seen in the ballroom, this man's suit was fully black, and was accompanied by a black shirt and collar. Coupled with his dark skin, it struck her that this man was a walking shadow, yet something about his kind eyes brightened the entire room.

"I am Arthur Ondorian, High Priest of Tandera."

Her mouth fell open. She then realized that her shroud was gone. She'd been too absorbed by the strange animal that she'd lost the concentration necessary to maintain it, and now she'd been discovered.

"I'm sorry, sir. I—"

"No need to apologize. Weston told me about you."

"He did?"

The man nodded. He was middle-aged, soft about the middle, and had a crisp, precise voice. "Dinner ended a little while ago, and Lord Grey was not sure how to find you in this maze of a building." The priest stepped forward, looking up at the heads. "The Trophy Room." He glanced back at the strange fox behind Aly. "That beast is the biggest prize in this room." Aly followed his gaze. "A creature from the Deep. A creation of the Canyon that lives nowhere else."

Aly shivered as she looked again at the animal's wild eyes. "What did you call it? A foxblood?"

The man nodded. "The perversion of a true fox. As the woodwolf is a perversion of a wolf. The Canyon takes something we know and twists it. These creatures are hard to kill. Do you know who killed this one? It was Lord Grey."

"Sir?" She blinked from the man to the beast. *Grey kills creatures of the Deep? Has he been there?*

Ondorian smiled. "Your tutor is a man of many secrets." He raised a hand. "And perhaps it is better if you do not ask him about this one. The memory is a difficult one for him, I think."

The man stared at Aly for a moment, until she felt obligated to speak. "Sir, should I go?"

"Ah, yes." He shook himself, as if coming out of a small reverie. "I will accompany you downstairs. You may resume your shroud if you wish."

This man was the High Priest. He knew more about the *Verad* than anyone, theoretically. Grey had said she could ask him her questions. *But can I? Why had the High Priest of Tandera come searching for me at Grey's request?*

"You have questions on your mind," he said as he lifted a hand toward the door.

"Are you a sorcerer?" she asked, unsure why this mattered more than her other queries, but hoping he'd say yes. She wanted to speak to someone who could Truthpull.

He shook his head. "I am not, but I have trained a few in my day, as Grey is training you."

"You have?" she asked eagerly, if somewhat stupidly. She

walked ahead of him into the hall, not shrouding herself for fear it would seem rude.

"Before I was selected as High Priest, I trained three men and one woman as sorcerers. I find the practice of perfecting Truthpulling to be one that requires a special kind of person. I do not mean the sorcerer. I mean the source." Aly glanced back at him awkwardly as she walked in the narrow hall. "The source, you see, is the one who risks much. It takes a man—or woman—without much to lose to become a source for a Master in training."

Aly had never considered that Grey had little to lose. He owned more than she could conceive of. "But the source has some control, right? They allow the sorcerer access to the truth inside them." She didn't want to think Grey was entirely at the mercy of her inexperienced and rather inept hands.

"That is not so much control as it is participation."

Those words failed to comfort Aly. "How does that work? He isn't a sorcerer."

The man behind her exhaled slowly. "You are asking the right questions, but I think the answer is better learned rather than explained. Ah, this way."

Aly made a face that he couldn't see. So much for answers.

They walked in silence down a winding stair she'd not encountered before. It spat them out of a hidden door at the end of the mirrored hall beside the ballroom. A shortcut.

"Come visit me this week at the cathedral. I will gladly answer more of your questions then, Alyana." He lifted a hand toward the other end of the hallway where a pair of doors stood open to the ballroom. Guests milled in and out of the doors. "Now, if you wish, you may shroud yourself again. I understand Grey's choice to keep you a secret. For now."

He nodded to her and walked away. His words spun in her mind, but she complied and draped her shroud over her once again. *Grey told him it was his choice to hide me?* In a way, it was.

But really, he'd *agreed* with her that invisibility was the best choice. *And what was that about it only being 'for now'?*

More questions for Grey.

As she rounded the corner into the ballroom once again, a new sensation struck her. The room buzzed with several dozen sources of energy—the guests. Above the mingling courtiers and statesmen, all luminous and full of truth, burned a source that surpassed the rest. She couldn't tell who it came from, only that it was there, in the midst of the crowd, making every other Truthwell appear dim in comparison.

She honed her awareness of the sources around her. Almost immediately, she knew Grey was near the back of the room. The familiarity of his energy brought a wave of comfort in the midst of a world where she didn't belong.

As she wove through the room toward him, she was aware of the one source that seemed so much deeper, so much brighter than the rest. She couldn't describe magical signatures as sound but they contained percussion-like patterns. They weren't tangible, but she could feel them like a fine, warm dust. They didn't really burn with light that she could physically see, but she *felt* them the way a man feels and sees a fire even with his eyes closed. They burned with a silent, invisible heat, with an intensity that only one like her could sense.

Then she found the person who belonged to the sun-bright Truthwell.

She spotted him not because he was taller, but because of his movement. A young boy with eye-catching red hair was scurrying among the guests, his tails barely flipping out behind him. Another boy was following him, or perhaps chasing him. Aly stepped around a pair of women to try and trace the boy's movement. Of all the people in the room, one particular person was emitting more energy than the rest. This boy.

Grey was standing off to himself when she approached. She dropped her sound shroud and coughed to announce her position. "Grey," she whispered, hoping not to startle him. He didn't even flinch.

"Aly," he said with a small nod. He emptied the contents of a wine glass and passed it off to a nearby server. He lifted his arm again, and she took it without hesitation this time.

She caught the edges of a real smile on his face as he led her toward the exit. "Who is that?" she whispered, then realized he couldn't see who she was pointing to. "The boy," she clarified.

"That is Prince Frederick."

Aly followed the prince with her eyes until he disappeared behind a group of courtiers. Grey tugged her along a bit.

"Good evening, Your Majesty," Grey said, startling Aly and drawing her attention forward.

Before them stood a man in a vivid red suit. A medallion hung around his neck and a simple gold crown, etched with the pattern of flames, rested on his head. The crown had a single red stone on the front. She was grateful at that moment that the King of Tandera couldn't see her gaping mouth.

"Good evening, Lord Grey. Until next week." The king gave a curt nod and a broad smile to Grey and turned away.

"Next week?" Aly asked, nearly breathless as Grey pulled her out of the ballroom. *That was the king!*

"Council meeting," Grey muttered, careful to keep his voice low as they walked by a few women chatting in the foyer. Outside the palace doors, he added, "You'll be here too, for the meeting."

I'm coming back to the palace? So soon? "Why do I need to come to the king's council meeting?" She still held his arm, even though they now waited in the courtyard for Grey's carriage. He made no gestures for her to let go.

"Aly, where I go, you go. At any rate, there's someone I'd like you to meet that day."

"Who?"

"The king."

6

On the way back to Grey's estate, he mostly batted her questions aside, his mind clearly elsewhere.

"Can we just sit a moment? Without any questions?" he finally barked, one hand resting against his temple.

Shocked, Aly closed her mouth. She watched as the city buildings shrank from grand stone structures to smaller wooden and plaster buildings, which finally gave way to fields. The gates to Grey's estate were lit by burning torches, and Aly felt, oddly, like she was coming home.

It had only been two weeks since she first stepped foot inside Grey Manor. How quickly things had changed.

Grey helped her out of the carriage, which she assumed was just his gentlemanly duty.

"Hungry?" he asked, his small smile present again.

"Yes," she admitted.

He led her to the kitchens, where the cook, Constance, sat knitting a blanket, as if waiting this whole time. Without a word, Constance rose and began a fire in the stove.

Grey pulled out a wooden chair at the small table and sat. "Now, I'll hear your questions."

Aly didn't waste a moment. "The prince. Is he a sorcerer?"

He leaned back, legs stretching out wide, one arm on the table, half facing the cook as she prepared a midnight meal. He looked tired. "No. What makes you ask that?"

"His energy signature is strong." *But the other sorcerers hid their Truthwells*, she reminded herself.

One of Grey's knees bounced. "Hmm."

"I thought perhaps he just wasn't shrouding his Truthwell, the way the other sorcerers seemed to. They had no signatures at all, which I thought was strange. I've never thought about shrouding just my Truthwell."

He appeared to drift away from the conversation. Aly tried another question. "Those paintings at the castle."

"Palace," he corrected.

"Whatever. Those paintings. They had angels in them, didn't they?"

Grey snapped his gaze at her. "Angels?"

"They floated in the air. They looked like angels." She tried to conceal her embarrassment. "The departed spirits. The *Verad* says they live in Theod's realm."

"Noticing art?" He nodded in approval. "Those were the sorcerers."

"Sorcerers?" she gawked.

An annoyed sigh was his response. "Yes, Aly, and angels are *not* spirits of the dead. The *Verad* says no such thing."

"You claim to know the text then?"

"You seem surprised."

He was teasing. It was late and she was so tired that she wasn't exactly sure what to make of it. "No, sir."

He shook his head. "Aly, I—never mind. Go on. More questions?"

She nodded. "Yes. You told Ondorian to come look for me. How did he find me in that huge castle—"

"Palace."

"How did he find me? And why did you tell him it was your idea I stay invisible?"

Grey pinched two fingers at the bridge of his nose. "He is the most knowledgeable man in the country when it comes to the truth. He's no sorcerer, but I bet he can sense magic like no one else. Not the way you do," he added when he saw her brows rise, "but somehow. You can ask him yourself when you meet."

"I was going to ask about that too."

"He's busy, but he agreed to meet with you." Grey's eyes were beginning to look heavy. He stared down at the table with a vacant expression for a moment. "I told him it was my idea so he wouldn't ask you about it. You and your mother seem to have your reasons for keeping you hidden, and I don't need to know what they are."

His tone sounded strained, as if offended. She watched her knotted hands as she spoke. "I always thought my mother wanted me to stay hidden because of my magic. Now that I'm here, I'm honestly not sure why she wants me to stay out of sight."

"A mystery, then." He narrowed his eyes. "I like a mystery. You could say it's my job to parse out mysteries."

"Your job? What exactly *is* your job? I thought you were on the king's council."

"That's hardly a job. It's a position."

He said nothing more. The question was closed. He had given her a small sliver of something she'd not known before, but he'd withheld the full truth. He was keeping secrets from her, and it seemed like he wanted her to *know* it.

How does this help build trust between us? She wanted to ask Arthur Ondorian how to access the *full* Well of truth inside of Grey. There had to be a secret to it. Something maybe even Grey didn't know. Just looking for more magic everyday was too simple an answer. It would be like looking for more air in the forest. Truthpulling was an art, and there were masters of this art. She'd seen some tonight, masked and hiding. Maybe Ondorian would have more straightforward answers next time.

They sat silently as Constance finished up a pot of soup. The vegetables were still fairly hard, but they had a crisp, fresh taste and were warm. Aly tried not to eat too voraciously.

Apparently, she failed.

"Good grief. We'll need to work on *that* too." Grey stood, stretched, and bid her goodnight.

Watching him go, she had a strange and sudden urge to follow. He'd dangled a secret in front of her, a woman who could become invisible. *Is he tempting me to follow, or demanding it?*

She downed a few more bites, thanked the cook, then disappeared out the same door Grey had taken.

His rooms were empty. She'd suspected they would be, but she'd checked just to be sure before leaving the house. Remembering her words about sneaking around the house while invisible, she waited until she was outside, then conjured her shroud.

The times she'd seen him in the mornings, he'd always looked exhausted. More than once, she'd been awakened near dawn by crunching gravel outside—the curse of a light sleeper. One thing was certain: this man did not sleep every night. She was going to find out why.

By the time she reached the stables, his horse was gone. She knew he rode Ruby more than any other horse, and as she recalled, Ruby had appeared tired that first morning they'd worked in the stables.

She had only ridden one of Grey's horses, a bay mare named Miss Turner. She grabbed up her skirts, wishing she'd had time to change out of her ballgown. *Guess we'll see what happens.* She hopped onto the unsaddled horse, her dress bunched up around her torso in awkward, unladylike poofs. There was little time to catch up.

She extended her shroud to cover the mare as well. Bareback was uncomfortable, so she added a little cushion of air between her and the horse's backbone as she nudged it into a gallop outside the barn. Her body began to flop dangerously, and her legs had no strength in them to hold her on the horse. Fortunately, she had magic. She crafted a spell to press her against the horse's back, ignoring the pain caused by the mare's spine.

Grey had only just passed the gate. He was not riding as hard as she was, perhaps not to draw attention to himself as he trotted by the few homes that stood along the road into Mardon. Pulling from the trees nearby, Aly concentrated hard on preserving her shroud, despite the ticking of her nervous heart.

A few nobles had moved to vast tracts of land outside of Mardon, perhaps to escape from the town's crowded conditions, and it was to one of these homes that Grey now rode. Aly followed at a distance, though she knew he could neither hear nor see her.

When he moved inside, she left Miss Turner under the cover of darkness beneath a willow tree, should her flimsy shroud fall apart as she moved farther from the horse. She really would have to learn to shroud from a distance.

Lights and shadows in an upstairs window indicated movement. Assessing the bricks, she considered edging them out toward her to make steps. She wasn't sure what this would do to the structure, and she didn't want to bring this house down while trying to be stealthy.

With energy from a large oak beside the house, Aly gripped the small indentations between the bricks and began to climb. She had never tried to move herself before, and she immediately began to fear falling as the ground inched farther away. Her magic made her body rise easily, lifted simply by the air and her mind's command. The fine material of her dress snagged on the rough brick, but she would worry about that later. Her biggest concern was trying not to fall. The tree was a strong enough source. She hoped.

Clutching the window ledge, she peered inside. Drawn curtains prevented her from seeing who was inside, but she heard two male voices. She had one way of knowing if it was Grey.

Eyes closed, heart hammering, she sought out the sources of energy in the room. As her mind found Grey's signature, she momentarily lost concentration on the shroud around her. She quickly rebuilt it, but she feared they'd heard her small frightened gasp.

Sure enough, a man Aly didn't recognize peeked out the curtains a moment later. She trembled, barely able to hang on despite her magic's help. He couldn't see her. He dropped the curtain and continued to speak with Grey. She thought she heard him say *shipment* but couldn't be sure.

As she hung there, considering how to let herself down, she became suddenly aware of one alarming thing: the tree's energy was about to run out. She hadn't realized how much she was using to hold herself up and to maintain her shroud around her body and the distant horse. One would have to go.

In her agitated state, her shroud dissolved. That was one thing she couldn't afford to lose, not when the man at the window would be back if he heard anything.

One option opened up to her.

She reached for the energy inside of Weston Grey and *pulled*.

With the power it fed her, she let go of the brick and floated gently to the ground. She released his energy and sprinted for Miss Turner. Covered once again in her shroud, she rode the mare at a full gallop all the way back to Grey Manor.

By the time she had walked the horse enough to calm her down, Aly could hear another set of hoofbeats approaching. Quickly, she led the mare into her stall, apologized to her, slid the door shut, and scampered off toward the house, where she fully planned to be asleep in bed before Grey could come check on her.

But as she neared the house, she realized Grey had stopped his horse by the front door. The night butler, Yates, was already leading the horse toward the stables. Of course. Grey didn't have to sneak into his own home.

Aly's heart beat madly on her way to her rooms.

Grey stood at her door, arms crossed, leaning against the wall.

With a deep breath, she dropped her shroud.

"Ah," he said. His small smile was gone.

An apology felt wrong, so she said nothing. Her hair was windswept. Her skirts wrinkled and snagged.

He pushed away from the wall and strode toward her with a strong step. When she felt certain he was going to backhand her, she cowered.

"I was wondering when you'd follow me," he said, inches from her.

"What?" she balked.

"I have been checking on you every night to see if you've followed me. After what I said earlier, I assumed I'd draw you out." Her expression made him laugh. "Aly, I've got an invisible woman living in my house. How can I *not* assume you'd follow me? Do you not have your suspicions about me? Surely you are not *that* naïve."

"Sir?"

He spun away from her. "If I tell you the truth, will you believe it?"

"How will I know? Sir?"

When he spun around again, she was even more surprised by his almost mischievous grin. "Will you not call me Weston? Or at least Grey?"

He was echelons above her in society. She had no right to call him anything but 'sir'. And, he was mad.

An exasperated sigh pushed from his lips. He walked toward her, a tired but determined look on his face. She backed away as he neared until she was against the wall.

"Grey," she finally said, turning her face aside in confusion. He stood too close. At the ball, his nearness had been a comfort. Now, it made her cheeks flame and her heartbeat soar.

"You're right. How can one person know when another is telling the full truth?" He leaned forward just slightly, then placed one hand on the wall beside her. "Alyana. I…"

She didn't want him to continue. She closed her eyes, startled and completely unsure of her ability to fend him off should she need to. She'd grown so comfortable around him so quickly. This was ruining it.

"Please don't," she mumbled.

He coughed. "I think you misunderstand."

Her eyes popped open. He was still close, but he was grinning again. The grin that said she'd gotten something wrong.

"You are beautiful. You are everything I should want."

"But?" She was surprised she asked it.

"But I was asked by Gevar himself to train the most powerful natural sorcerer I could find. Part of that agreement, part of the training, is to let you into places I let no one else. To give you access to *all* of me." He dropped his hand, which Aly noticed was fisted. "Well, in the magical sense, that is." She squirmed. "You followed me tonight, which means you don't really trust me."

"You *wanted* me to follow you."

"I figured you would at some point. That is not the same thing."

"You don't trust me either, despite what you've said. You checked on me every night? Just because you *figured* I would sneak out after you. Paranoid?" She crossed her arms as he spun away, fuming.

The king wanted him to train a sorcerer. That means the king either really likes him and wants him to have a good bodyguard or thinks of him as expendable. Ondorian had said to train a sorcerer was to risk one's life.

"All right, don't tell me what you do at night," Aly said, stepping toward him. "But tell me something that will help me trust you. Tell me this. Why is a twenty-year-old on the king's council?"

His eyes widened. In the dimly lit hall, Aly couldn't read his expression well. With a wave of her hand, a candle sconce behind her head burst to life, illuminating Grey's face. His mouth was hard, flat, unsmiling, but his eyes were blazing with what might have been fear.

"I suppose I can answer that. Most people know the reason, after all. The ones who haven't been living under a rock for sixteen years, anyway." His small smile flickered again. "I was a soldier, briefly. Signed up when I was your age. Infuriated my father. His best source for magic was leaving him." As he spoke, his face darkened. "Went north, to the border. I was foolish and young. I wanted to be stationed at the Canyon, to prove my bravado." He scoffed. "There's a reason the army pays those soldiers so well. *No one* in their right mind wants to take that post. Let's just say I made a name for myself up there. For some really strange reason, I was good at killing Canyon beasts. It made people think I was…holy or something." He cracked his knuckles.

Aly recalled the foxblood in the Trophy Room. Ondorian had warned her not to broach this subject. *Oops.* "So the king picked you because you were such a valiant soldier?"

His jaw flexed and he turned his body like he wanted to end this conversation. "Gevar awarded me a medal of valor, yes. When I had served my three years, I returned home, sick of the blood and the terror of the men up there. But I wanted to keep fighting the Canyon. Gevar found out and offered me a position in his personal guard. I told him I was through getting paid to hold a gun and wait for evil to strike. That's when he offered me the position on his council. The war hero turned pacifist." Grey shrugged. "I've served fourteen months on council, and in that time, I've said probably five things, but he hasn't kicked me off yet."

Aly yawned. Her dress was not warm, and she was stealing energy from the air to keep from shivering.

"I'm boring you."

"No," she said, then had to cover another yawn. "I'm just tired."

He looked her up and down. "Get some sleep. From now on, don't follow me."

"I won't."

"Can I trust you?"

"I haven't killed you yet."

His smirk eased her tense shoulders. "True enough. Good-night, then." He walked down the hall. "Oh, and Aly? I'm going to buy tickets for the symphony tomorrow night. Ondorian is a bit of a music fanatic, and I want to make sure you've been to at least one before you meet with him. Is that all right?"

A smile curled one half of her lips. If this was how their arguments resolved, she didn't think it was so bad after all.

7

Grey said he wanted to be able to see Aly's face when she glimpsed the cathedral for the first time, so she didn't shroud herself as they rode through town, hoping no one would see Lord Grey riding around with a young woman.

She tried to ignore his stare and looked out the window of the carriage. The spires were visible from afar, but buildings were erected close around the cathedral, concealing the façade until they were right before it.

As the massive cathedral popped into view around the edge of a neighboring building, Aly's mouth fell into an open smile. She turned her head to see the top. It was so much bigger than she could have imagined. The small abbey in Kitrel was a cottage compared to this structure that reached towards the heavens.

Grey chuckled at her.

"It's incredible," she said.

He stepped out of the carriage and left the door open for her. Before she exited, she covered herself with her shroud. As they entered the vaulted stone space, the air became cold. Aly stared in wonder at the ceiling so high above them. She wondered how it didn't collapse in on itself. Her neck began to ache as they walked the length of the nave.

She finally looked down when she realized a man was waiting for them at the front of the large church. It was Arthur Ondorian, and he was wearing his priestly robes.

After brief pleasantries, he dismissed Grey and bid the invisible Aly follow him.

They passed through an arched doorway, up a short staircase, into a string of smaller rooms at the back of the church, all open and set with nothing more than a desk and chair. Study rooms for the priests.

They stopped at the end of the hall at a wooden door, the only one that was closed. On the wood had been carved a small phoenix, the emblem of Tandera.

"You may drop your shroud, now," he said.

She obeyed, and he smiled at her.

His study was small and bare. A cot sat in the corner. An ancient copy of what looked like the *Verad* lay open on his desk. There were two chairs, and he motioned for her to sit in one.

"Do you like music?" he asked.

A flash of Grey's face filled her mind. She nodded. The priest turned to a large object on the floor by his desk that she hadn't noticed. It had a strange flower-shaped trumpet protruding from the top. He touched something, and the deep resonance of an upright bass and cello filled the room. The priest smiled when he saw her incredulous face.

"I call it bottled music! A gift from the Duchess of Ingard on her last visit. Actually, from her sorcerer, but all the same." He nodded at Aly. "The magic is almost as fascinating as the fact that I can have the sounds of Carlos Tintero in my very room."

"That's *magic*?" Aly leaned forward. "How?" Her mind began to spin. A shroud could silence sound. Could there be a spell that could trap sound and then release it elsewhere?

"I can see that you are filled with questions." He smiled again. "That is good. I always want my students to be curious. Curiosity for the truth is the best place to begin. After all, it is going to be something that you have to study on your own. I can answer your questions, but the text will be something that becomes yours. Do you have your own copy?"

"My own copy?" She looked at him, bewildered. The *Verad* was enormous and thus expensive. Renna had never been able to afford something like that.

He held up a hand and moved over to a small shelf. He removed a book and held it out to her. "Take it. You will need it. Every sorcerer must learn this book."

She accepted the book. "Everyone who does magic knows this entire book?" she asked, surprised at how anyone could learn all that the book contained.

Ondorian frowned and sat back down. "No. Far from it. And that is why there is much twisted magic in this world. But all you need to know to conduct magic is in there."

"I've studied it some. In Kitrel. When I had the chance." She ran her hands over the smooth leather. "There's so much I don't know."

"It will come, in time. No one can learn it in a day."

She glanced again at the music box. "I can learn to do *that* just based on what's in here?"

"You can learn to do infinite wonders, Alyana. The challenge is knowing if you should."

"What could be bad about *that*?" She pointed at the strange, melodic box.

The priest shook his head. "The invention is not bad, nor is the magic that spills back this blessed music to my ears. But anything good can be twisted into something bad. When the sorcerer made this, I doubt very seriously if the man or woman considered what might happen if a person's voice could be manipulated to forge an identity or if the magic of the Deep could begin to take hold of this and turn its beasts into sentient creatures—or at least ones with the power of magically enhanced speech."

Horrors of talking foxbloods sprang into her thoughts. "Some can perform magic without knowing what's in here," she tapped the *Verad*. Her question, she hoped, was clear enough in her words.

Ondorian sighed. "The Canyon has a unique power. One that acts like a source. You understand?"

"Like the way I use Grey as a source?"

"Like that." The priest's kind face fell a little as he spoke. "The Canyon is a strong source. I am told the river there is one of the world's strongest sources. Some sorcerers have sought it out for this reason. Everyone who has pulled from its power has been corrupted by it." Ondorian rested a hand on his copy of the *Verad*. "Theod warns not to put trust in things that will fail. A river may feel like an endless source, but it is not."

"The river, sir?"

He didn't give a direct answer. Instead, he turned and read a line from the text. "Trust not in princes. Trust not in the earth. Trust not in dreams."

Aly gripped the book. She wasn't exactly sure how the river at the bottom of the Canyon and the prince of Tandera had anything to do with each other. "We aren't supposed to trust our rulers?"

Now the priest actually chuckled. "Oh, certainly not all of them, but that is not the principle here. Simply that power is not always underneath a crown." He winked at her.

He remained silent a moment, and Aly assumed she was to pose another question.

"Sir, I do have some questions. They're not exactly about the text. They're about Grey, some things that he said."

"Why did you not ask him?"

She blushed and looked at her hands. "I thought that you

might understand better, sir." He nodded appreciatively and waited for her to continue. "Does Theod gift some sorcerers with *more* magic than others?" Grey had said she was a special case.

"Ah. Curious where you fit in among all this?" He lifted a hand vaguely toward the tiny window. "Indeed. Theod makes some men into architects capable of building structures like the one we sit in. He makes others poets or composers. He makes some sorcerers. But the architect, the poet, and the sorcerer must still study and learn and improve."

Not really an answer. Again. Aly was beginning to wonder which questions she could receive a straight answer to. "Why is it that people have so much more energy inside them? And why are some people brighter than others?" She thought of the young prince.

Ondorian nodded, as if approving of this inquiry. "To your first question, when you pull from the energy inside of a person, you are accessing something greater than what is inside a rock or a tree. A rock, you see, cannot speak or know truth. Its truth is summed up in its existence, nothing more. A person, however, can know, believe, and love the truth. Or, as is often the case, a person can reject and hate the truth and believe instead a lie. It is a difficult thing to understand and even more difficult to explain. As I cannot see this magic as you do, I cannot offer much more in answer to your question." Aly fought the urge to roll her eyes. "As to your second, purity makes some Truthwells, as you say, brighter. Not purity in quality or in goodness, but in devotion to the truth. Lies do not merely weaken those with magic—they weaken us all. The *Verad* explains that to believe a lie is to craft your own reality, one that does not exist. Your work with Grey will prove most beneficial to gaining a better understanding of this phenomenon. Perhaps you can add your revelations to the Canticles."

"What is that?"

"Ah, what is that? You are as green as he said. The Canticles are a collection of writings from sorcerers throughout history. They contain personal accounts of Truthpulling across the ages. Enlightening reading, if you find the time. I am certain His Majesty would grant you access to the palace library for study. For now, something I would like for you to study this week is the fourteenth book." He leaned forward and tapped the cover of the text in her lap. "Do not start at number one. Well, certainly you may, if you wish to learn about the history of the world and the beginnings of the Canyon, but to find the answer to your question, read book fourteen."

"Yes, sir." She assumed by now that if she asked another question, he'd dodge it with a philosophical response or give her more to study. She wasn't sure what else to say.

"Few people have the gifts you have, Alyana. Use them well."

She squirmed in her seat. The responsibility sounded too great for someone like her. She knew too little.

"Do not be worried about Theod's choice. Now, it is your responsibility to learn that book."

As he led her back out into the awe-inspiring nave, she felt a bit disappointed. She had expected a more direct approach to this tutoring session, but she was extremely grateful for the copy of the *Verad* and was excited to begin poring over it.

"Thank you again," she said.

He gave her a small bow. "Might I suggest a walk through the city this afternoon? Better to do it alone so you do not have to hide beneath your shroud, yes? I take it you have not been to the city much?"

"Not at all, sir. Except in a carriage." She knew enough from those three rides to know that the main street out of the city was called Broad Street. If she got lost, she could ask someone how to reach that street. From there, she could find her way back to Grey Manor. The idea of a walk through the city sounded exciting.

"Protect that," the priest said with a small nod at the book in her arm.

She thanked him a final time and walked out the front doors of the cathedral, visible to all the world.

A nobleman. The High Priest. And in a few days, the king. Aly was quickly leaving behind the girl from the cabin in the woods.

With head high and eyes bright, Aly walked into the great city. In the cathedral's square, a boy was selling newspapers emblazoned with the headline: *King Attends Pauper's Funeral.* She smiled to herself. She'd be meeting the *king* soon.

This was the city of the king—now her city.

"When he enters, you will rise," Grey instructed as the palace servants left him and Aly alone in a fancy little room with high windows and elaborate chandeliers. "If you wish, you may remove your mask for him." Grey looked down at the mask in Aly's hands.

The green and silver mask had been on her dresser when she woke up that morning. He'd sneaked into her room while she slept—a feat, considering what a light sleeper she was. It was as if he was proving to her that he could sneak better than anyone, whenever he wanted. The nights he left and returned on thundering horse hooves were nights he'd wanted her to hear him.

The mask was a sign that Aly was progressing in her mastery. Not the elaborate mask of a true Master, but a mask nonetheless. She held it with eager, slightly trembling hands.

"If I wish? Do I not *have* to show my face to the king?" She sat on a plush couch in a fine dress. Her life was becoming more and more full of nice dresses. She didn't hate it, but she hadn't mastered the posture of a noblewoman yet either, which made wearing these dresses a reminder of who she was not.

Even on the second trip, the palace stole Aly's breath. The Sunrise Room, as the palace servant who'd let them in had called it, was decorated to look like the morning sky. Pale orange drapes framed the windows, and blush peonies bloomed in vases stashed all over the room.

Grey stood beside a pink marble mantle. His waistcoat was buttoned today, and he wore the beginnings of a cold-weather beard. "You do not have to. At palace events, there are plenty of sorcerers who never remove their masks. He understands their culture of secrecy."

She did not miss the word *their* and the way it placed a barrier between them.

"Culture." Aly mumbled the word, aware that she was a member of a culture she'd never even known existed. She didn't quite fit in a noblewoman's dress, and she didn't quite under-stand the need for the sorcerer's mask. She was attempting to wear both today and feeling like a hen in a goose pond.

But as she stared down at the sequined mask, almost reptilian with its green and silver colors, she couldn't bring herself to put it on and step back into the nothingness that she'd lived in for sixteen years. *I'm done hiding.*

"If he wants to meet me, why doesn't he want to *see* me?"

"He'll see you." Grey pointedly eyed her dress, making Aly squirm.

"You gave me the mask but no cloak."

Grey cocked his head back a little. "That's right." Aly stuck her chin out, waiting for his explanation. He laughed. "Aly, we'll only get maybe five minutes of the king's time, then you're with me the rest of the day. No sense making you wear that hideous cloak just for five minutes. We've got plans after this."

"Plans." That wasn't much of a reason.

"Today I thought I'd show you *art*. Mardon Museum. Two o'clock."

She blinked at Grey, suppressing a smile. "It's a good thing people can't see me when we go out. People might start to think you're courting someone."

At that moment, she wished she could disappear. His eyes pinned her to her seat. She'd meant it as a joke. She rarely had a chance to jab at Lord Grey the way he jabbed at her, but her words carried too much truth in them to be just a joke. She quickly became absorbed again with the mask in her lap.

He took one step toward her.

Just then, the doors to the room opened and a servant stepped in. His white and gold attire was free from stain and wrinkle. "Your Majesty, the King of Tandera." He swept an arm backward as he bowed out of the way.

Aly hopped to her feet, her hands fumbling to pull the mask down over her face to hide the hideous blush that had flooded her cheeks. Her pulse was out of control.

In strode King Gevar. His beard was full and reddish and perfectly trimmed. He had an air of confidence and formality that intimidated Aly. She tried to back up as he marched forward, but the couch behind her prevented it. She nearly toppled backward.

The king stopped, then he broke into a hearty chuckle. "Why, I do not mean to frighten you. Have a seat, have a seat." He waved a hand at the two of them. "Grey." He nodded and took a seat in an ivory winged chair.

And just like that, Aly was sitting across from the king.

He crossed his legs and placed his hands in his lap. He looked so comfortable, so at ease.

Aly's back remained so stiff that she never touched the cushion behind it. Her face began to sweat beneath the mask. It was several seconds before she remembered she could lower her body temperature. This she did, pulling a tiny amount of energy from Grey.

"You are Grey's new sorcerer. He tells me of your rapid progress."

He's spoken to the king about me? She stared out dumbly from the small eye holes. *Am I to respond? How does one speak to a king?*

The king glanced at Grey, who now sat on the other end of the couch from Aly, close enough that she could feel the couch tilting her toward him. "A chatty one, eh?" Gevar asked.

Grey spat out a laugh. "You have no idea, sir."

"Indeed? Well, I find that a good thing, as sorcerers are concerned." He winked at Aly.

Winked? Kings winked?

"We average folk like being informed of what the finer race is thinking, considering we do not have the pleasure of observing their expressions." He smiled at Aly, his enjoyment of the conversation almost contagious. "A silent sorcerer is a much more frightening thing. Come, tell me, how do you like this impertinent young man?" He didn't bother to conceal the mischief that curled one side of his mouth.

Aly glanced at Grey, having to turn her head all the way to see him. "He is most generous, sir."

"Oh, come off it. We all know Grey is nothing of the sort." The king leaned forward, a conspiratorial gleam in his brown eyes. "He is a rogue, is he not?" Aly blushed behind her mask. "Ah, not willing to say an unkind word. Also an admirable trait. Grey, I do believe you have found a most rare and honorable woman."

Found a woman. Like I belong to him. Aly felt Grey's eyes on her, though she didn't turn to look at him.

"Indeed, sir. She's the best thing that's happened to me in a long time."

She froze. Heart thundering, she contemplated what he could mean. He'd never, save in his expression moments ago, showed any sign of thinking of her as more than a student or an employee.

"I can see that," Gevar agreed. His kind face stared knowingly at Grey. Something about his eyes gave her pause. They were full of *pity*. What did the king know about Grey that Aly did not?

"Sir, I am honored to meet you," she said, trying to fill the strange silence and prove that she could speak to a king.

Gevar was not what she had expected. He had the commanding presence of a king but the affable demeanor of a father and friend. Besides Grey, Aly had never really spoken to men, other than a few of the farmers and shop keepers around Kitrel; to them, she had been just the weird girl who lived in the cabin in the woods.

"It pleases me to hear you say that. Not all sorcerers feel the same." Gevar eyed Grey again. "An idealist also? My dear man, where *did* you find her?"

She missed Grey's response. *There are sorcerers who don't respect the king?* She must have missed a question posed at her, because the room grew quiet as the king and Grey waited for her to speak.

"Sorry, sir, I was too startled to think there might be sorcerers out there who are not pleased to meet you. Can you repeat the question?"

Grey covered a cough and the king's brows rose. She'd misspoken. Fortunately, no one could see the way her cheeks flamed in embarrassment.

The king sighed and stood. "My dear, it was so nice to meet you."

That's it? Well, he is *a busy man.* She stood too, offering a small, awkward bow. The mask nearly fell off—she hadn't secured it properly. She grabbed the curved edge to steady it. As she straightened, she pushed the mask up and off her head.

"Alyana Barron, sir. The pleasure is mine."

King Gevar stepped forward, a hint of delighted surprise on his brow, and took Aly's hand, raising it up to his lips. She stood, stunned, as the king turned to go. He'd touched her as if he did not fear her at all.

"You will have your ring in no time. I believe it with my whole heart."

"My ring?" She hadn't meant to say it aloud, and she paled as the king simply chuckled at her question. *What is he talking about?*

A smile broke across her face that didn't fade as the king walked away. But as he left, she saw his final glance at Grey. *That is definitely pity.*

When she turned to Grey, he was staring at his feet.

He's hiding something. Aly vowed to find out what.

8

"The ring of the Master Sorcerer," Ondorian explained, walking with his hands clasped behind his back along the river's edge. The path followed the Cresen River through the heart of Mardon. Stars peeked out from behind low clouds, and pale street lamps lit the way.

The High Priest liked to take late evening strolls along the Cresen, when his priestly duties were mostly over for the day and he could walk without as many people interrupting him for blessings or inquiries about the *Verad*.

He'd had no time for their regularly scheduled meeting that week, therefore had agreed to speak with her during one such evening stroll. She walked without her shroud, at Ondorian's suggestion. It wasn't abnormal for the High Priest to answer people's questions or offer small lessons to inquisitive parishioners, so no one would consider it odd for him to have a young woman accompanying him.

"Comforters, as you have no doubt learned," Ondorian continued, "are the lowest among the sorcerers and also the most common. Some believe the magic once handed down by Theod to the final son of the first family was much more powerful than it is today. But I believe this is a misconception created by the fact that so much of the magical blood in the world today is simply mixed with the blood of the nonmagical. The much-diluted magic in a Comforter is but a trace of what it could be."

Aly pulled on the energy in the water nearby, warming her body to combat the bite of the season's first cold snap. Ondorian wore a heavy woolen cloak, dark grey and plain. Nothing like the fine, embroidered ivory cloaks of the Master Sorcerers. She asked him again if he wanted her to warm him up.

"No, thank you. I prefer to live life at the mercy of *my* blood. Theod made me incapable of magic, and I want to live with what he's given me."

"Does that mean I shouldn't help others by using my magic on them?"

He shook his head. "No. It is a *gift* to use your talents, Aly. I just do not want to pamper myself unnecessarily with something I cannot sustain."

"You would never hire a Comforter, then? Or a Protector?"

"Indeed not, but I digress. You asked about the ring His Majesty mentioned. The Master Sorcerer distinguishes himself —or herself, as the case may be—by creating for himself an item made by magic, something that could not exist without magic." He paused to look at her. "Sorcerers may claim to be humble creatures, but they maintain their hierarchy as well as any society. The Comforters are barred from wearing the mask and cloak. Of those who wear the marks of the most elite sorcerers, only the Masters wear this piece of jewelry, often a ring, that sets them apart from those not capable of bending matter to their will."

A stinging breeze rolled in off the river, and Aly pulled harder to warm her body. The result was that the air around her grew even colder. "Sorry," she muttered, realizing her own comfort was decreasing that of the High Priest. She let go of her spell and felt the rush of frigid air across her frame. At least her magic wouldn't add to the chill.

The priest noticed her shiver and opened his mouth to say something, then reconsidered and kept walking.

After a moment, Aly's teeth were nearly chattering. She'd forgotten what it was like to live without the comfort of magic. Her body and her senses wanted to reach for the magic that would warm her, but she shut her mind off to that possibility. Just for a bit longer, she chose to suffer the cold.

"Dear girl, you may warm yourself," Ondorian said after several minutes of silence. "It is not wise to grow so cold when your body is not accustomed to it, as mine is."

Fingers shaking, she reached a hand toward the water, but instead of drawing warmth from the water, she tried something else. A strand of water rose and wiggled in the air like a fish. Aly crumpled her brow and tried to force the water into a circle. The water moved *around* in circles, but it did not form a complete circle. When she glanced at Ondorian, his brows were high and he wore an amused smile.

The water splashed back into the river.

"I thought I'd try," she admitted, pulling a wave of warmth into her freezing limbs and chest. Her trembling muscles melted. As a quick breeze pushed against the priest's cloak, she mumbled, "I'm sorry."

"You are kind, and that will take you far. Now, what else shall we discuss before our time is up tonight?"

She had one other thing on her mind, but she wasn't sure Ondorian had the answer.

"We've talked about the shadows that mix with the light I see when I'm Truthpulling. They're only in people, and you told me those were the lies that pollute the truth inside of us." He nodded as she spoke. "What about secrets? Do they affect the light too?"

Ondorian pinned her with one of his piercing stares, as if he could read her mind. "Secrets are not always lies, and lies are not always secrets. The darkness inside of us is both a choice and a curse. Lies, too, are often a choice, when we craft them, but can be a curse when pushed on us by someone else. Lies deepen the darkness and make the truth harder to see. Those whose Truthwells manifest to you as—how did you say it? Shadowy?—perhaps are living within a lie. The difficult thing is that most of us do not *know* when we are believing lies. Otherwise, we would abandon them. If only we all had your ability to see this light and dark as you do. Then perhaps we could rise above the lies that plague us. This, too, is part of your gift."

Grey had said this man could see the truth in ways most men could not. She wasn't sure how to pose a question about this, but she said, "Sir, sorcerers are not the only ones capable of knowing what is true and what is false."

"Ah. You are wise indeed. Theod did not leave us helpless against the dark."

"How do you sense what is true?"

He glanced sideways at her, a curious expression on his face. "Did Grey explain to you what a reckoner is?" She shook her head. "I am a truth reckoner. It means I can say that which is true when asked a direct question. I can expose a lie only if the right question is asked."

Aly stopped walking. "Really? How does that work?" She'd never heard of a reckoner.

Ondorian smiled with pressed lips. "Another of Theod's mysteries. I can see you are not pleased with that answer. Suffice it to say that as High Priest, I have certain *privileges* that others do not." His smile took on a mischievous nature, and Aly couldn't help but return it.

"You speak of the shadows within Truthwells," Ondorian continued. "Do not go seeking that darkness, Aly. Pull *only* the light. I suggest you do not go seeking the secrets that plague you either. If they are secrets of truth, you will know them one day. If they are secrets of darkness, you do not want to know them."

As they strolled back toward the cathedral that perched on the river's bank, Aly wondered if Grey's secret was of lies or of truth.

~

Two months later, Aly knew the way back from the cathedral like it was the road to her former cottage in the woods. Mardon's tight streets and odd smells were home now, as were the halls of Grey Manor.

Her *Verad* no longer traveled with her to her meetings with the High Priest. She memorized a passage and discussed it with him each week. Ondorian would then task her to attempt magic based on the words of the text.

"Trust not in the earth," she muttered, one hand lifted toward a fallen tree in Grey's back field. The tree responded to her by lifting itself up. The branches groaned and cracked as the tree moved. When it was righted, it hovered in the air, roots exposed, dropping small chunks of earth as Aly pondered what to do with it.

Grey had said it was *in the way*, but she knew this was just an excuse to have her practice moving it. A few horses roamed this back field but had spooked at her magic and galloped away. Few people ever came this way.

Aly marveled at how the magic waited for her command. Using the *Verad* to shape her spells had changed so much of what she'd known about conjuring.

Pulling from the nearby forest was easy enough, but when she used words from the *Verad* to shape her desires, it was like a billows to a flame. The magic brightened in response to the ancient text. Not in giving more energy, like the deep Well of energy in Grey or the bright fire of power she'd seen in Prince

Frederick, but when guided with *Verad*, the energy of a tree could last much longer without killing the tree, and it seemed almost eager to do as she commanded.

Ondorian was right. The *Verad* really did govern magic, and not just because it outlined *how* magic came to be and *why*. The text itself *shaped* magic. It was like she'd been a river spilling out of its banks for far too long, and the *Verad* provided a channel, cut with precision, through which her magic could flow. Her spell held the tree a moment longer, then with a small flick of all her fingers, she bade the tree split apart into firewood.

A deafening *snap* boomed across the field. Aly flinched. The tree was now in an enormous pile of evenly splintered logs.

"Someone else can come pick these up," she said aloud, satisfied that she'd saved someone a lot of effort, then she shook her head. "Wait. That's stupid." With hands lifted, she pushed the logs into the air, forming a neat line. "The will is strong," she quoted, needing only a sliver of a verse for this spell. Somehow, though she could do the magic without the *Verad's* words, she almost always used them now. The effort expended was much less, and the ease with which she could pull magic from the items around her much greater.

The logs danced through the air all the way down the field, across a partially frozen creek, into the already half-full wood shed. The resulting pile was so large that it filled the shed and spilled in great heaps all around it.

"Good enough," Aly said, ready to see what Constance had cooked for lunch.

As she approached the house, Grey walked out to meet her. He wore a heavy winter coat over his customary suit. He'd been in town that morning; he'd left her behind to deal with the tree, and because he'd said his business was confidential. Aly disliked his secrets, but she'd promised him she'd never spy on him again. Somehow, she'd find out what he was hiding.

"I heard an awful racket. What happened?" Then he noticed

the overflowing wood shed. His gaze drifted back to her, incredulous.

Aly fidgeted, waiting for him to say something. Her hands were warm despite the frigid wave of air caused by her magic when transporting the wood. The heavy cold of winter had come, and she was grateful to see the woodshed overflowing, though part of her wished she could have sent the wood all the way to Kitrel and into Renna's tiny cabin. She hoped her mother was warm and well fed, that her knees weren't giving her too much trouble.

"Aly," he finally said, "you're incredible."

Grey's breath steamed the air. His face was familiar, though he now wore a full beard. *It makes him more handsome*, she thought. She'd tried her hardest to memorize his every expression, so she could know his thoughts without hearing them. Just now, she detected something in his gaze that she hadn't seen before: *regret*.

What's wrong? she asked silently, her mental voice still a bit unassertive and small.

This skill had been a strange one to discover. Ondorian had opened her eyes to so much, including the mysterious and surprising fact that Aly could speak to someone's mind, if she was using that person to fuel her magic. The first time she'd tried it on Grey, he'd spilled his morning cup of coffee.

Magic could do so much more than she'd ever known.

Grey could not answer her silently, but he could hear her. He allowed her, at Ondorian's encouragement, to practice this form of communication, but he made it clear he was never a fan of her voice appearing in his mind.

His frame shuddered slightly. "You have learned all you need to be *my* Protector."

The way he emphasized *my* gave her pause. She recalled he'd told her that she would reach Mastery quickly, and that she would be moving on after that. But she hadn't thought much of it in the past two and a half months. She'd had too much to learn, too much to do to think of what would happen *after.*

His secret? Could it have something to do with what will happen when I reach Mastery?

He looked away, appraising her work at the wood shed again. "But there is one more thing you should master before my work is done."

Your work is almost done? she asked him with her mind. *You mean I'll reach Mastery after this last task?*

"It isn't a task, Aly." His words were shorter than usual. "It's a skill. And, yes, if you can do this, you should easily be able to make a ring out of whatever you choose."

Her face lit up.

The ring of a Master Sorcerer. No matter how often she'd tried since that night Ondorian had explained it to her, she'd never been able to fasten a band of water, dust, flower petals, or even ash that would hold for more than half a second. The most she could do was make a circle, then as soon as she touched it with her hand, it would fall apart.

She strode up to Grey. She was finally feeling a bit of the cold around her, and she pulled a tiny bit of energy from him to warm her body. She did this so easily now that she barely even knew it. Grey, too, was unaware. "What do I have to do?"

In the short time she'd been at Grey Manor, she'd left the girl from Kitrel behind. She knew Grey better than everyone else she'd ever met, save her own mother. Ondorian, the High Priest of Tandera, was a friend as well as a mentor. She'd learned to use word magic. She'd met the *king.* She'd even spoken with the queen and the royal family once. She'd attended symphonies and plays. She'd learned to eat with propriety and grace, and she'd become more accustomed to the dresses supplied by Grey's tailor, though she still wore pants and a blouse on most days to allow for whatever magic she needed to practice—including moving her body through the air.

She'd grown stronger than she ever thought possible.

He reached one hand out and squeezed her shoulder. He was a tutor, a colleague, a friend. Some days she almost hoped he saw her as more than just a student or employee, but she had to hide these thoughts. When he touched her like this, she had to fight even harder. *Did his hand linger, or is that my imagination? Does it make him warm the way it warms me?*

"I think it's time we practice stopping bullets."

Her chin jerked back in surprise. She'd heard the lore. Grateful that Renna had taught her to read, she had spent her time devouring Grey's impressive stash of novels and history books when she wasn't needed elsewhere. The books contained both facts and fantasies about sorcerers. Some stories told of magical power that could stop a bullet. The history books were less supportive of this as an actual power, considering the use of pistols and rifles as weapons had been rare until the last century. According to the novels she'd read, this kind of power resided only in the strongest sorcerers in the world.

Grey sensed her hesitation. "You'll master this. I've no doubt." She smiled weakly. "We will start tomorrow. I have more business in town this afternoon, and I would like you to spend that time preparing. Bullet diversion is difficult, even for the most skilled sorcerer, and I'd rather not die." He offered a small smile.

"We won't be aiming *at* you, surely?"

He laughed. "No, but the amount of energy you'll need to pull from me will be more than anything you've tried before. It'll have to be accessed *very* quickly."

Aly's face paled. Just when she'd begun to feel comfortable Truthpulling from Grey, now she was tasked with this. "If it's possible, I'll do it. I'll learn." She wanted to believe it.

Grey narrowed his eyes. "I believe you will, but didn't Ondorian tell you not to say things like that?"

Aly frowned. "Yes." The High Priest had told her that she

couldn't *create* truth just by speaking it—that was a dangerous path to tread. But he'd also highlighted again and again the importance of believing in her own ability. *Is it so wrong to simply tell myself I can do it?* "But I just…I want to believe I can do it."

"You *can,* but it might take some time."

"Then we'll practice as long as it takes." Suddenly, she wanted to be the one capable of stopping bullets, of protecting a king's councilman, even perhaps the king himself. She didn't really want that kind of responsibility, but she wanted to at least be *able* to do it. The desire was tangible. Nothing would stand in her way.

He *humphed.* "Yes. I suppose we will." Despite his words, his tone suggested time was somehow not on their side.

Aly yelped as Grey fell to the ground. Again.

She rushed to him. Hands shaking, she reached for him. He opened an eye and playfully swatted her hand away.

"I'm all right." He eyed the bullet hole in the makeshift target they'd set up, which consisted of a board propped against a pile of earth.

Her trembling hands withdrew to cover her mouth. Breath swirled in the air between them. Grey stood up, grunting.

"Please sit down. I don't like watching you fall."

"I don't like falling." He tilted his head at her.

"Oh, like I can control it!"

He grabbed her arm before she could storm away. "Aly, you *can.* This time, don't use me. See if you can draw power from something else. See if that changes anything."

Aly perked up. They'd been practicing stopping bullets for a week. No telling how much ammunition they'd blown through as Aly failed and failed again.

All she'd managed to do so far was cause a bullet's path to divert. That had begun to be problematic, considering their target was fairly small. She'd blown a hole in a nearby tree and sank three bullets into the earth beyond their target. It was a good thing they were deep in the woods on Grey's property.

"Or we can try again tomorrow," he suggested.

"No. I will get this."

He nodded. "Yes, you will." He checked his watch.

"You've got a meeting tonight, don't you?" She meant his late-night outings, the ones they never spoke of directly. He simply eyed her, giving no answer. "I'm fine to keep trying, if you are." She glanced at his dirt-stained pants; at least he'd left his fancy suits behind for these practice sessions. In these old pants and a plain white shirt, he looked more like the men from Kitrel, which, oddly enough, was less familiar to Aly than the fine-suited Grey she'd come to know.

He waved a hand at her. "Go on then." As she stepped back, he reached down into the dirt and picked up the pistol. He blew on it twice to remove some dirt, then added one bullet from a stash in his pocket.

She stiffened in anticipation of the shot.

"There you go again," he said. He wasn't looking at the target. "You tense up."

She exhaled, relaxing her shoulders. "You're right." She held up a hand to indicate he should wait and closed her eyes. For a moment, she pretended she was standing in the market square in Kitrel. She remembered the exact place she'd stood while mending the crumbling bridge. The memory was crisp, worn into a sharp rut in her mind.

She'd been nervous too that day. She'd been afraid. She'd been worried people would see her perform magic. She'd had to choose the wellbeing of others above her own fears. In that moment, she'd been able to search out the sources around her and connect with the river, despite its distance. Ondorian had told her that magic intertwined with thoughts so intricately that for a sorcerer, they were one and the same. This was why she was able to warm herself as soon as she felt cold, and this was also why she hadn't been able to conjure proper magic around Grey that first day, when her mind had secretly been attracted to him. Magic was directed by the mind—a terrible thing considering how wild one's thoughts could be. This was why word magic was much more precise, much less dangerous.

She searched for a phrase she hadn't tried yet. All the texts she'd memorized over the past few weeks had seemed pointless when it came to stopping bullets. When the *Verad* was written, bullets hadn't existed. She had tried all the usual phrases that allowed her to bend nature to her whims, but bullets were not natural.

What else is there? Stopping bullets *was* possible, according to Grey. The Royal Sorcerer could do it, and in order to be considered a true Master Sorcerer, she had to conquer this skill.

Magic, like science, kept morphing as the minds of the Masters tried new things. That musical recording in Ondorian's office was one example. The sorcerers of old had never had to learn to stop bullets, but when the challenge arose, the magic rose to meet it. She could *do* this. She just had to figure it out.

She'd never be good enough to create her ring if she didn't.

She still wasn't looking forward to having to wear the mask and cloak of the Master Sorcerer, but contrary to what she'd thought at first, the disguise was not the same as hiding in the obscurity of the woods. The mask was the mark of talent. To wear one was to be who she'd always dreamed she could be: a sorcerer who didn't have to hide her magic. To wear one was to *belong*.

Aly reached for Grey's energy burning nearby. The rhythms of it, the shape of it, were familiar. She could wade into it now with ease. But as she welded her mental magic with the truth inside of him, there was always a moment she felt unwelcome.

She always felt a strange *pushing* against her, as if the magic were trying to overwhelm her, the way a wave can either bury or buoy.

She only knew to handle this odd sensation by grasping the magic and *pulling*. She focused her thoughts on the gun, on the bullet inside, then nodded to Grey, eyes still closed.

The shot made her jump.

"Grey!" She ran to him again, her mind riotous with the fear that she'd somehow made the bullet change course and hit him.

He rolled over on the ground, revealing a thin, bleeding scratch on his cheek where he'd landed on a small rock. He groaned. "Can we start again tomorrow?"

She grabbed the gun and tossed it aside. With one hand, she pressed on his shoulder, clutching the loose fabric there, and the other she placed on his cheek. Using his own energy, she sealed his wound and eased the pain inside him. "Better?"

He rolled to his back on the cold, hard earth. "Yes." For a moment, he lay there, eyes on the clouds. She sat beside him, her arm just touching his. Quickly, she pulled her arm away.

Apology after apology ran through her mind, but she couldn't voice any of them. He had agreed to this. He had more confidence in her, as indicated by his words, than she had. At least she could relieve his pain.

But why is he still falling?

"I'm afraid to pull harder," she finally admitted. He sat up, his body close. "You fall down as it is. If I pull harder, I'm going to… I could strip you."

A chuckle burst from his lips. "Now that I'd like to see."

Her brows rose in horror. "I meant—"

"I know perfectly well what you meant." He leaped up, then held out a hand to her.

She wanted to burrow into the dirt to hide. Truthstripping was deadly and wasn't something to make jokes about. She placed her hand in his, and he yanked her up, a grin on his face as he caught her. She was too young for him. He was too *close*.

He smelled like dirt and the rich, tangy smell of the oils he put in his beard. There was a hint of the smell of Grey Manor on him too. The halls had a sweet wood-polish smell about them that hung on her clothes as well.

"Aly," he said, his voice huskier than usual. She could barely breathe. "Don't be afraid." He let go and stepped away.

Her breath flew from her mouth, exploding into the cold air. He ran a hand over the back of his neck.

"Tomorrow?"

"Yes. Tomorrow." He dropped his hands. "Yvesy has a showing tonight."

"In town?"

Grey nodded. "It's a private showing, actually. Another of Gevar's commissioned pieces."

"A private showing *at the palace?* And you get to go?"

He covered a small cough. "The king always asks a small group to attend events like this. He's generous like that. Do you want to attend?"

Laughing, Aly shook her head. "Why would anyone in their right mind say no to that?"

Grey smirked. "It's questionable whether you're in your right mind." He indicated the dirt on his clothes.

"That's not fair!" She swatted his arm, then immediately felt foolish for her action. But he just chuckled.

"Just teasing, Aly. Stopping bullets isn't exactly easy. If it was, all sorcerers could do it." His brows rose. "If you like, you can wear the sorcerer's cloak tonight."

The invitation was one of confidence—he finally trusted her to be his *public* sorcerer. His Protector. But she had been picturing another pretty dress, not the enormous, nearly winged drapery that was a sorcerer's cloak. And with the cloak came the mask.

But this was also what she'd been working toward. This was the path she'd chosen. Master Sorcerers, those capable of more than just heating and cooling, wore the attire of their own nobility. She was one of them now, though she still didn't know any of them.

"Okay."

Tonight, for the first time, she would wear the clothing of an elite sorcerer. Tonight, she would be recognized as the nobility of a different court.

9

As the carriage rolled toward the palace, Aly focused on Truthpulling only a sliver from Grey to propel them. Aly still wasn't used to the lack of clopping horse hooves on the cobbled roads, but she had grown accustomed to the way it felt to be in a constant Truthpull. Just months ago, she'd spent most of her time with her mind closed off to the energy sources around her. Now, sitting in the cab with Lord Grey on her way to the royal palace, she continually left her mind open to the sources nearby. She'd discovered that the entire world held a faint golden glow to it, each item burning in its fascinating way with tiny dust-like particles.

But the longer she left her mind open to the light, the more she began to detect the shadows. Aly, now more acquainted with the way truth magic lit her world, also saw the darkness that swirled behind it. Ondorian had said lies could pollute the truth. Based on what she could see, lies affected everyone.

Grey's energy thrummed its familiar pattern against Aly's consciousness, and with it she turned the carriage wheels at an even pace. "I can see why noblemen like the idea of horseless carriages. It tells the world they've got magic protecting them."

To keep them both warm against the chill of her magic, she used a bit more of Grey's never ending Well.

"Indeed," Grey agreed. He wore a sharp black suit and his hat sat on the carriage seat beside him. "It's sort of like showing off. Noblemen are good at that."

Aly fiddled with the hem of her ivory sorcerer's cloak, which she hadn't yet fastened over the silver dress she wore. She'd wanted to make sure Grey saw the dress, the same one she'd worn to the palace the first time. The cloak's wide, pointed shoulders and oversized hood would take getting used to, as would the tall shoes she wore under her dress.

"You ready for this?" he asked, nodding toward the bright mask in the seat beside her.

"I guess I was born for it?" she replied, her voice rising as if in doubt.

He chuckled. "You were. It's a bit of a shame though."

"What is?"

"That you have to wear that bag over that dress."

Her face lit crimson.

He continued, voice more formal, "But you need to take your place among the sorcerers. Staying invisible isn't the answer anymore. Anyway, when you're invisible, I can't see your dress either."

Now her whole body broke out in a nervous sweat. Pulling magic made her warm anyway, and she couldn't handle the look in Grey's eyes—though it's exactly what she wanted, the reason she hadn't fastened her cloak.

He was just a teacher, an employer. A *nobleman*.

She wasn't sure if sorcerer nobility was considered the same as courtly nobility. One was based on inborn ability, the other based on wealth. They shared one thing, however; they were both based on power.

Before they turned into the palace courtyard, Aly fastened her cloak and donned her mask. The world grew shaded at the edges, and her breath warmed her face. Walking up the palace steps, her heart hammered in her chest. The wide points off her shoulders created space between her and Grey. She had to walk carefully in the tall shoes, and she hoped it came across as graceful, measured.

The crowd was smaller than it had been the last time she'd come to the palace, only about two dozen people. The king sat chatting with a glass of wine in one hand and a pipe in the other. He laughed out loud at something the other man said, then lifted his glass at Grey and Aly. He appeared so casual this time, relaxed.

Aly felt terribly out of place. *How am I here, among such a small crowd, with the king?*

Grey nodded at her, as if confirming that she belonged here, then, he turned aside and walked to speak to the other guests. Among the milling courtiers were two other cloaked sorcerers.

Breathe, she told herself. The room was warm, so she used Grey's energy to cool her body. He talked so easily to those gathered here. She stood silently, not sure who to talk to. The other two sorcerers were engaged in a rather intense conversation, and as much as she wanted to approach them, she couldn't even move.

"I am glad to see you again," said a deep voice behind her.

She spun to face the King of Tandera. His neat, reddish beard was parted over a warm smile. A small bit of tension released from her shoulders. Strangely, his was the only other familiar face in the room. She'd spoken to him once, and only for five minutes.

He knew who she was. Of all the people she would meet at events like this, only Grey and King Gevar would ever know who she really was beneath the mask and cloak. Somehow, that was comforting, in a startling sort of way.

She bowed gently, not wanting to lose the mask or stumble in her shoes. "Delighted, sir." She realized as soon as she spoke that no matter the disguise, her voice would give her away as a woman. She still wasn't fully in agreement with the secretive nature of Master Sorcerers.

"I hope you enjoy the show," he said, and walked away.

Aly took her seat in the second of two rows of chairs, beside Grey. The shoulder of her cloak just touched his shoulder. Every time she shifted or he recrossed his legs, her cloak brushed against him. As the draped paintings were brought in and placed on stands, she had to force her awareness away from that point of fabric.

The paintings remained veiled for several more minutes, the conversation still bustling among the seated guests.

"Where is Yvesy?" Aly whispered to Grey.

"Probably with Carolyn."

"The youngest princess? Why?"

Grey chuckled. "She's rather demanding, and she made him promise to show her how he mixes his paints. She likes to know how things work. And Elise, the older one, is a fine painter, for her age. Yvesy gives her private lessons."

Wow, must be nice to be royal.

The door to her left burst open, and in rushed the youngest princess in a ruffled dress, followed by the strawberry-haired Elise, and finally the flaming red-haired prince. His Truthwell's brightness filled the room, and Aly had to look away.

"Does the prince have a sorcerer of his own?" Aly asked, watching the boy again as he walked dutifully to his seat on the front row, beside his mother. His friend, the darker-skinned boy, sauntered to his chair, as if glad the entire room was watching him.

"No," Grey answered, but he was prevented from saying more because the man of the hour had arrived.

Yvesy, grey-haired and thin as winter icicles, stepped into the room.

The king stood, which made everyone else follow suit. When

the crowd again took their seats, the artist nodded at two gloved attendants standing beside one painting. They lifted the cloth.

A collective mutter of admiration fluttered through the guests as they viewed a portrait of the three royal children. He'd captured them so perfectly; it was as if they stood at the front of the room.

He really is good, Aly thought, finding it hard not to squint through the eyeholes in her mask. It would take getting used to. Fortunately, as she was now more used to seeing the Truthwells around her with her eyes open, she realized the mask provided a rather pleasant bit of shade against the room full of burning energy. Perhaps there was more to the face coverings than a desire for humility and secrecy.

The second painting was of a horse, majestic in early morning sunlight.

Grey leaned over and muttered, "The king's horse."

When the short showing was over, many of the guests circled around Yvesy. Aly would have liked to speak to him as well, to offer her own words of appreciation for the beautiful art he'd created, but she stood at the edges of the group as Grey exchanged cheers and pleasantries with his fellows. He, too, wasn't much of a conversationalist at these events, but he had no problem approaching those around him.

"Hi," said a small voice.

Aly blinked down at the youngest princess. "Hello."

"You're a sorcerer."

"Yes."

"That's—I mean, that is fascinating. I like magic."

"What do you like most about it?"

The girl considered the question a moment. Grey peered over his shoulder and spotted Carolyn talking to Aly. He smiled and turned back around. "I like it because it can *do* things. My father's sorcerer made me a clock out of items from my room. It works, too."

"That is amazing."

Carolyn shook her head, her curled hair wiggling. "No. It is just magic. Amazing would be if I could make one without magic."

Aly smiled. "Maybe one day you will. People make clocks all the time."

The princess laughed. "All the *time*. That's—I mean, that is funny. You are funny."

She's too smart to be eight. "Thank you."

"I want to make a clock one day. I want to make all the things magic can make. But I do not have magic." A forlorn expression crossed her face.

"But you have a brain; I bet yours is capable of anything."

Her face lit up. "That's—I mean, that is what my father says." She bounced away like that was the end of the matter.

For a brief moment, Aly's heart ached from an old wound, the wound left when her father had decided he'd rather remove Aly from the world rather than raise her. One person had loved Aly enough to parent her, when the task was never meant to be hers. Renna had saved her.

I miss you, Mama.

The art showing was a short event, and people started moving toward the door sooner than Aly had anticipated. She still hadn't spoken to the other two sorcerers. They hadn't approached her either, which disappointed her. She was the new one, the one who didn't know anyone. They could have introduced themselves.

Grey stopped beside her. "Ready?"

Aly grunted. "I didn't talk to them."

Following her gaze, he sighed. "The one on the left serves Lord Alexander. Also a councilman. Rather stuffy, but extremely wise. His sorcerer is pretty well the same. I don't speak to him much myself."

"You claim to not talk to many people, but you talked all

evening." They bowed once more to the king and queen, then exited the room.

"I talk because I am expected to. I didn't say I enjoyed it."

"You laughed the whole time."

"A practiced skill."

His hand hovered near her back, his energy signature telling her what her eyes couldn't see. He wouldn't touch her like that, not while she wore the sorcerer's garb. *Would he?*

"The other sorcerer, you would like. He protects Duke Wyndall. Before that, we fought together at the border. Likes to poke fun at Alexander."

Sorcerers fight at the border too? She halted. *Of course. They'd be the best soldiers up there.* A shiver of guilt flushed over her. *Should I fight at the border?* She had power that the average man—that Grey—did not. He'd fought. He'd protected his country from the growing darkness.

"When will I meet them?" she asked, forcing her mind away from visions of leaping foxbloods.

Their footsteps echoed through the vast foyer, and they were out in the night once again before he answered. "Soon. Remember how I said there was an event you could attend if you mastered your magic? Turns out, I actually need to leave a few days early. One of my business contacts just moved to a city along the way, and I need to meet with him. It will add a few days to the trip."

"And?"

He ran a hand over the back of his neck, and Aly narrowed her eyes at him, wondering what bothered him. "And I wanted you to have that ring before we left." He smiled at her.

"So basically, I need to get cracking on that bullet stopping?"

He chuckled. "Exactly."

Their carriage was parked in a line at the edge of the courtyard, and Aly summoned it. It was still strange to see it moving on its own, but she enjoyed the thrill of knowing it was *her* magic that moved it. She'd been toying with summoning her breakfast, her clothes, any item she needed to grab. It was just too fun.

"When is the mysterious event?" she asked as they climbed in. She wondered why he hadn't mentioned what this event was yet, an event where being a Master was, somehow, imperative to her attendance. Her mind played out all the worst possibilities. A trip to the Canyon.

"I need to leave in two days."

"Two days?" To his mind, she said, *Does that mean I failed? I don't get to go?* There was no way she could master bullet-stopping in two days.

"I would like you to go anyway. As my official Protector. You're ready, Aly."

Her heart lifted. "But I'm not a Master yet."

"I think you're powerful enough to go to this. I wanted you to be…well, I honestly wanted to show off that I had a Master as my Protector. It was a dumb idea, Aly. You're a powerful sorcerer. Who cares if you get to make your own Master's ring?" He sounded like he was convincing himself. "And we're going to Virienne. To a wedding."

A wedding? She laughed aloud. She'd been expecting danger. Some sort of gauntlet to test her ability.

Now her heart flipped. She'd never left the country, and she'd never been to a fancy wedding before. An embarrassing question filled her mind. *Am I going* with *him or just with him?* She didn't dare ask. Instead, with her eyes out the window, she said, "Virienne! What part?"

"The Sapphire Coast. It's warmer there, even at this time of year." A new smile brightened his face, but he too kept his gaze out the window.

Her lips cracked open in astonishment. "Will I be wearing this?" She lifted her arms and pulled off her mask.

Now he stared at her. "Is that a yes, then?"

"It's a yes," she said, which seemed eerily like she'd just accepted an invitation to go *with* him. She'd figure that part out later. Aly wasn't frowning as they wheeled back to the manor house in the carriage.

That night, shortly after the long chiming of midnight, Aly heard hooves on the gravel. As soon as she heard Grey's galloping horse approaching, she knew something was wrong.

He rarely hurried home, and he was returning earlier than usual.

Aly had spent her childhood afraid that someone would discover her magic and come to punish her or steal her away from her mother. This had trained her to waken at the slightest sound. Strangely enough, someone *had* come to take her away because of her magic.

A lingering confusion from a dream drifted out of her mind as she sat up in her large four-poster bed. She never slept well on the nights Grey left to conduct his secret meetings. It was her job to protect him, but he still refused to take her on these outings. Each time he left, when the rest of the house was asleep, she feared he wouldn't return, and somehow it would be her fault for *not* being there.

Her room was a mess as she packed for the trip to Virienne. She grabbed her ivory sorcerer's cloak from the chair where she had tossed it and raced down the wide wooden stairs. Grey used the front door on these nights, presumably because it was far enough away from the staff quarters not to wake anyone upon his return.

He crashed through the front door in a huff, his face not surprised to see Aly's cloaked form descending into the foyer.

"Aly!" He rushed to her.

"Are you hurt?" She started examining his body.

He grabbed her shoulders. "No." His voice was so firm and raw that she stilled. His eyes were tight and fierce. "On my way, a messenger...I—come, sit down." He led her to a bench just below the enormous painting of life and death. Her blood vibrated in her chest, arms, and hands.

"Your mother."

"What about her?"

"Oh, Aly, I'm so sorry. She...she passed away two days ago."

Aly's chest caved in, and she slumped against Grey. The cavern that opened up inside her threatened to consume her. He pulled her into him, wrapping his arms around her, tentatively at first, then with purpose.

As she cried, he whispered over her head. "I met the messenger on the road. He was riding hard to reach you, but his horse was already weak. I dismissed him to take the message to you myself." One hand stroked her back. Aly was entirely numb, not even registering his touch. "The man, he said...Aly, he said she died from violence."

She pushed up and looked Grey in the face. *How could he possibly say that? No one on the planet would want to harm my mother. She is the kindest, mildest woman alive. Or was.* Aly shook her head, hoping to rid her mind of what he'd said.

He leaned down a little to look at her. "There's more, Aly."

Swatting at him, she stood and pressed the heels of her hands to her eyes. There couldn't possibly be *more*.

Behind her, Grey sighed. "This is difficult. I don't even know what to do with it myself. I—"

"What? You don't know how to take news of *my* mother's death? Don't be cruel. You can't pretend you care about a woman you don't know." Her eyes were already puffing so much she could barely keep them open. The tears were so *hard*, so forceful. She could barely control her shaking body.

"No." He hung his head. "Not that part. I'm sorry, I truly am. But the other part, the *reason* she was killed..." A deep breath preceded his next words. "Your father. He found out where you had been living and it appears he came there to kill you, but found only your mother."

His words made no sense. "My father left me as an infant. That's why Renna fled after my mother died."

"No, Aly. Your father has been searching for you for a very long time. He heard word of how a young, pale girl living with a brown woman saved the bridge, and he tracked down your cabin. Renna was the only one there when he arrived."

Shaking her head, Aly wiped away more tears. "No." She repeated it several more times. "Why would he care now? Renna said he was an evil man. That's all I know about him. *Toss him!*" She rarely used this mild curse, but the word had a nasty satisfaction about it as she spoke of her father.

Grey stood and walked around to see her face. "Do you not know who he is?"

"Some foul man who didn't want his daughter."

"The messenger said the man had left a very clear indication of his identity when he, er, left your mother. I'll spare you the details, but you need to know who he is. Your mother never told you?" She tried to spin away from him, but he reached, gently, for her forearm. "His name is Dimitri Patrenko, the Royal Sorcerer of Bulvarna."

Aly glared up at Grey. All her life, she'd known only one thing about her father: that he had not wanted her. Renna had fled Bulvarna after Aly's mother's death because Aly's father had attempted to dispose of her and Renna had wanted to get away from him as well as the Canyon and its evils. End of story.

"The Royal Sorcerer of Bulvarna? Like, the one who serves the queen?" *My father is magical?*

Grey nodded.

"Well, toss everything then!" She spiraled out of his grip. The cloak hung open, but she couldn't care less about her nightdress underneath. Her mother was *dead,* and her father was the most powerful sorcerer in the entire country of Bulvarna. He'd tracked her to Renna's cottage. To *kill* her.

"He'll come for me here."

"He doesn't know where you are."

"But he'll find out."

"No, he won't." He sighed in frustration. "The wedding. Maybe you shouldn't go as a sorcerer. It would be safer if people didn't see a new sorcerer. Word could get back to him."

Not really caring about the wedding, she lifted her hands. "Fine, I'll just stay invisible. Forever." *That's why Renna hid me,* she realized with a start.

"*No,* Aly." Grey stepped toward her. "There's another option." His hands grasped her upper arms, gentle but firm enough that she didn't yank away from him. "As my guest."

His eyes were steel, his determination as sharp as her anger. He was mad, too. He'd not lost his mother, but he *felt* something strong and deep. "You'd be safe. Safer beside me."

Aly shook her head. "No. I'm dead. Mama always said he was an awful man. She fled because he tried to kill me, and maybe he wants to finish what he attempted sixteen years ago. Mama's not here to protect me anymore."

"No, but I am."

His words should have shocked her, but she was numb. He was just being kind. If her father ever found her, she certainly would not survive—not when the man had almost a century of practice and was powerful enough to serve the queen of Bulvarna.

Her head snapped up. *What if I became that powerful?* Though the pain was real and the grief overpowering, she resolved to do one thing: become strong enough to be offered the position of Royal Sorcerer.

"When he comes—and he will—I will be ready."

10

Aly, holding her dress with trembling fingers, stepped out of the carriage in Virienne. With her other hand, she accepted the help of an escort, grateful for his support as she stumbled onto the cobblestones. She hoped he couldn't feel her tremors, but her hand was visibly shaking.

They can all see me, Aly thought, struggling to control her rapid breathing. Grey exited the carriage behind her, and she could almost feel his eyes watching her. It was a bold move, him bringing her to this wedding as a guest. But to bring her as a sorcerer was an even greater risk now that her father was on the hunt for young, female sorcerers serving nobility.

She would hide in plain sight. It had seemed brilliant, until she'd seen the dress Grey had ordered made for her.

The music of violins greeted the wedding guests. Two young women dressed in black sat on iron chairs, bowing and swaying with their music as they played. Aly relaxed as she heard the soothing melody.

The young escort leading her toward the white-walled estate had a smooth face and wide eyes. He smiled at her and said something in Viriennese. Aly smiled back, letting him lead her past the musicians toward the open double doors. Grey walked behind them, his presence loud and bright in her mind.

Tonight she would be acting as his distant cousin, a young woman seeking exposure in high society. She'd disliked the idea, which she suspected was to keep the gossip down, but hadn't had the energy or the sense to argue for a different story. The only thing she cared about now was becoming strong enough to survive if and when her father ever caught up with her.

She would have her Master's ring. Soon.

Thick scents of flowers mingled in the cool, salty air. Blooms dripped from every possible surface: the doorframe, the banister to the upper floors, the mirrors, and the candelabra.

As she entered the house, warmer air drifted over her, washing some of her jitters. Their hosts no doubt kept a Comforter, who was responsible for keeping the house at the perfect temperature for the event.

Aly glanced in a huge mirror draped with white flowers. Her makeup-decorated face was foreign to her, and her dark hair was swept up in the common style. Grey had hired someone for the job as Aly could not have accomplished it herself, not even with magic. This world was still new to her, though she'd lived in it for three months now. In it, but not quite a part of it. Tonight, when she should have worn the sorcerer's garb and been introduced as part of that world, she was wearing a different disguise.

She was fully visible to all in order to remain invisible to one man: her wicked father.

Aly glanced tentatively at the boy leading her into the party. He was just doing his job, but she wanted to relish the fact that he could *see* her. Their hands were touching. She was not a sorcerer tonight, and she was not a ghost tonight.

But the boy holding her hand was not the reason for the heat in her cheeks. It had everything to do with the bright red dress hugging her body, and perhaps a little to do with the fact that Grey had been the one to order it.

Grey had been overly generous with this one. The other dresses he'd commissioned for her were of a plainer sort, less colorful and more in the Tanderan style, which favored a slimmer silhouette and paler colors. The Virienne style, however, liked bold colors and daring necklines. All the women here had dressed to suit the Virienne style, made popular by their young Princess Redonna, and Grey had wanted her to fit in, which, contrary to his intentions, made her feel more conspicuous than ever.

As she stepped from the house onto the sunlit balcony, a few heads turned her way. Her cheeks flamed.

"Tanderan," whispered a woman into her husband's ear. Aly caught the woman's eye and the woman nodded politely.

Red was the color of Tandera. Of Tanderan *royalty* specifically, but anyone from Tandera could wear the color as long as it differed from the royal red. Aly's dress was a warm scarlet, bold as blood. For a person who'd spent her childhood hoping *not* to be seen, this color was almost too much; she began to have a difficult time swallowing as more and more eyes glanced at the bright dress. At her.

The first terrace overlooked an even larger second terrace that had an unobstructed view of the sea. Aly smiled, thinking this was the most beautiful place on earth. The banister overflowed with woven flowers. Candles flickered everywhere. The ocean sparkled in the distance.

Men and women from across the continent had gathered for this wedding. A Viriennese duchess, niece of the king of Virienne, was marrying a Referen nobleman. Many important families had come, including King Gevar and his family. And somehow, Aly, a girl from Kitrel, was walking among them. Tonight she could understand, just a little, how Queen Isabelle must have felt that first time she attended an event with Gevar.

Prince Frederick and his sisters had arrived a few carriages before Grey's. Gevar and Isabelle were here, too, but Aly knew they would be sampling the best chilled wine in a private room until it was appropriate to be introduced.

The young escort deposited Aly near the top of the stairs on the terrace, nodded once to her, and spun to walk back into the house to escort another guest. Grey stepped up beside her. Aly's pulse thundered. Below her, royal guests and noble courtiers and at least three cloaked sorcerers milled about, sipping wine and finding their seats at the u-shaped table sprawled with greenery and tall candles. Aly had thought tonight would be her chance to finally speak to other sorcerers, to find her place among them. Instead, she was here as yet another young courtier, a little-known cousin of Lord Weston Grey. Perhaps she would at least try to talk to one of the sorcerers.

The head chairs were reserved for the bride and groom, though Aly noticed two small tables with a few chairs set on a makeshift dais to the side of the larger table.

"Those are for the other kings in attendance. One for Gevar and one for King Lucien of Refere. So they won't have to sit on the sides of a table," Grey said, following Aly's gaze. He lifted his elbow. She took it.

"You're sure Kassia wasn't invited?"

Grey stiffened. If Queen Kassia of Bulvarna had been invited, then Aly's father, the very man they needed most to avoid, would be here too. "Gevar had no knowledge of her being invited, and the king would know. Virienne and Bulvarna are not exactly friends." Grey tugged her arm a little closer. He had not touched her often since the night he'd informed her of her mother's death; he'd only touched her to help her out of the carriage or onto the boat that brought them to this island. She did not pull away. But playing the role of his cousin, she wasn't sure how close she should walk, how delighted she should feel at being near him. She'd wanted so badly to enjoy this wedding, but those hopes had been spoiled with the news he'd brought her that awful night. Her place beside Grey was not as his date, but as his cousin, in a ruse to keep her father off her trail.

She nodded at him. Her father was not here. She would be safe.

A trumpet blared and Aly jumped. A man announced Grey's name, then the false name they'd chosen for her to use throughout the evening. She'd never been announced at a party before. It was maddeningly embarrassing, not only because she lurched forward too quickly and stumbled into Grey, but because hardly anyone noticed her at all. Only a few faces turned up from their conversations and their wine.

Not surprising, she mused, fuming in an effort to quash the riotous discomfort inside her. She was visible, *very* visible in this gaudy red dress, and still no one looked at her, the unassuming girl from Kitrel. The nobody. The pain of this realization hurt more than she'd expected. She glanced down at the bright dress. It flowed out at her waist and hugged her chest, even though there wasn't much to hug. Thin sleeves like clusters of flowers peeled away from the neckline. *Even in this, I'm invisible.* Grey had still not said anything about her appearance either, which had disappointed her more than she wanted to admit.

She pressed away the ache inside her, forging it into anger. That was easier than self-pity; a sorcerer had no time for self-pity.

The wedding ceremony took place during the meal, which Aly found strange, and was entirely in Viriennese, a language Aly had never heard. She watched with a smiling face as the couple traded items throughout the ritual: a beaded headband, a shoe, and a crust of bread. When the crowd laughed, she forced a chuckle too, trying to look like she knew what was happening.

Each course was ushered in on covered platters as the priest explained something of great importance. This exempted Aly from having to talk to those seated around her as she ate, for which she was grateful. She wasn't in the mood to dodge questions or find a way around telling a lie—even if she spoke the false name they'd chosen for her, her magic would suffer. However, one of the guests nearby wore the cloak and mask of a sorcerer, and she couldn't help but glance at the mysterious man —she was certain it was a man due to his size—throughout the dinner. Her chair was far from the head of the table, one that put her back to the happenings but in plain view of King Gevar's table. She hated that she had to crane her neck to the side to watch the wedding, so instead she spent much of the time staring at the back of Prince Frederick's head.

The boy, at only twelve years old, still drew her curiosity and her attention. His magical energy outshone everyone else's at the party. Grey's magical signature was familiar to her, so she could focus on it easily, but the prince's was vexingly bright. She could hardly look away, even when her eyes focused down at her plate. His magic was lustrous like fine gold, nearly tangible in its billowing grace. She had never thought magical signatures were truly visible, but his shone bright enough that she wondered how everyone here didn't shade themselves from it as from a second sun.

Purity makes them shine brighter, Ondorian had once said. *Not purity in quality or in goodness, but in devotion to the truth.* The others present ranged in brightness. Grey was not as bright as the woman across from them but was brighter than the youngest princess. Perhaps young people burned brighter than those who had seen the horrors of life. Then again, the youngest princess emitted a rather dull light. At only eight, maybe she had not learned enough of the truth to burn very brightly at all.

By the end of the meal, Aly's neck was stiff and her stomach was much too full. The Viriennese people added sauce to everything. By now, the sun had disappeared beyond the horizon and only a warm light lingered at the edge of the sea as the newly married couple took to the dancefloor. The stars peeked out, and torches burned along the balcony and under the upper terrace.

Grey was engaged in a conversation with a Referen count on his opposite side. Many people moved toward the dancefloor, and the four masked sorcerers either remained at the table or wandered off to converse near the balcony's edge.

As the dancing began, Aly slipped from the table and into a firelit alcove. Though she longed to be seen, she felt more at home in the shadows. The dress, when she'd first put it on, had made her feel like royalty, but she looked nothing like the women here; these ladies were used to wearing clothing like this and idling among kings. Their posture and the way they moved spoke of the years of training that made one a true courtier. If Grey's jabs were correct, everything about Aly shouted her lack of court experience. Every time someone looked at her while she ate or while she walked, she sensed their valuation of her, their derision. She was not one of them.

In the alcove, Aly slipped into invisibility and breathed a sigh of relief. She never thought invisibility would be a reprieve.

She chose darkness and shadow.

The paintings she'd seen that first night in the palace made more sense now; the most powerful were the least visible. *Power is best when paired with humility*, said the *Verad;* hence, the culture of cloak and mask among the most talented sorcerers. Aly recalled Ondorian's words that the sorcerers, too, maintained a hierarchy among themselves. She pondered if this was true humility.

People walked by without so much as a glance her way. *No,* she thought, *invisibility is true humility.* The cloak and mask were symbols of *power,* written into history as symbols of humility. A grand façade.

She wished Ondorian were there. He too wore a robe as a symbol of humility. Of piety. *How is that any different?* Perhaps it *was* good to wear something that set them apart. She wasn't sure she could ever fully understand the long history of magic and humility and the ways it had both clashed and coalesced over the years. What she knew was that both sorcerers and those without magic were essentially the same—humility was unnatural for both.

She looked around for somewhere to go, somewhere she could pass the rest of the evening without bumping into anyone. Grey wouldn't notice her absence for a while. Since that night in the foyer, he'd been careful to avoid looking at her more than was absolutely necessary.

The lower terrace overlooked a cascade of white homes that reached to the seashore. Aly walked to the edge and breathed in the sea air. She'd been to two dinners in the palace at Mardon, but this was more intimate, more beautiful. Maybe it was the dancing. Maybe it was the sea air and sunset sky. She'd never seen the ocean before, and its endless expanse mesmerized her, soothing away the hurt that had clung to her every waking hour since she'd heard the news of Renna's death.

She's gone, Aly repeated again in her mind. She'd spent her life having only one parent. Now that her father had surfaced, he'd taken her mother from her. She'd thought she couldn't hate him more than she had as a child. She'd been wrong.

Her long-buried desire that he would appear one day and want to meet her had been crushed with the news that he wished her dead.

As she stood at the edge of the terrace, these thoughts polluted the momentary bliss afforded by the ocean view. Being the daughter of one of the world's strongest sorcerers, she too had been gifted with great power. Perhaps she could defend herself, and someday avenge Renna's death.

She gripped the stone before her. "You will regret the day you find me," she said aloud.

Aly glanced down at the seashore far below. A pair of dark figures, barely visible in the evening light, splashed in the shallow water, their laughter reaching all the way to where Aly stood. If she had been conducting the weather herself, she couldn't have created a more beautiful evening for this wedding. She was happy for the couple, who had left the dance-floor and were receiving guests.

Aly's mind wandered to dreams of her own wedding. In Kitrel, she'd been fearful that no one would ever want the strange girl from the woods. She'd feared that once a man found out about her powers, he'd flee. Instead, the first man to find out about them had sought her out. Hired her. Taught her. Asked her to accompany him here.

She glanced over her shoulder and spotted Grey. His face was half-concealed by the crowd, but she could feel his presence as clearly as the stone railing under her fingers or the dress on her body.

From the comfort of her invisibility, she stared at Grey. His face, though plain, had grown more handsome to her in the past three months. He wore a suit better than most of the men at the wedding. His posture was kingly; his smile, infectious.

He'd held her.

He'd seen her cry.

And he'd promised to keep her safe.

Before the news of Renna's death, he'd invited her *here*, to this wedding, as his official Protector. Now, he was trying to act as her protector. Since they'd met, she'd assumed he only saw her as a student or an employee; but maybe she had been ignoring what was right before her. She thought back to his quick glances in the carriage on the way to Virienne, the way he'd held her hand as she climbed out of the carriage, the delicacy and the distance he'd allowed her, giving her space to grieve. He hadn't even suggested they practice stopping bullets.

Grey lifted his chin and scanned the crowd. After a few passes, he turned his attention back to the woman in front of him. *Is he looking for me?* The possibility warmed Aly's cheeks.

Perhaps she could cut a door in the walls she'd erected around herself. He was a wealthy lord, and all reason told her he could never want her. She was too young—though she'd known of several girls in Kitrel to marry at her age. She was penniless. She was a sorcerer. She'd thought her initial attraction to him had been because he was kind and because he'd actually noticed her. She'd never had that happen before.

But what if it is more than that?

She closed her eyes and focused on his beaming energy. The bright truth from the young prince burned nearby, but she forced her mind to ignore it. She'd been too harsh with her magic these past days. Grey let her access his truth, and she'd been sloppy with it out of anger toward her father. A terrible and dangerous offense.

With her mind, she pulled gently on the truth inside him, opening it like a window to let in a breeze, without using up the breeze. It responded. In the moment before she commanded the magic to act, she felt that she held an ocean of pure gold light.

Strangely, she had nothing to command. No need to use magic. She fueled her shroud with the stones beneath her feet— a tiny bit of magic—but there was nothing else she needed to do.

Then she thought of something. It was a gamble, one she might regret forever. With the bit of energy she'd pulled, she formed words in Grey's mind.

Do you want to dance? She opened her eyes to watch his reaction.

His head snapped up. He was looking in her general direction but couldn't see her. She walked over to the alcoves under the upper terrace and dropped her shroud.

When he spotted her walking toward him, his face lit a fire in Aly's stomach. It wasn't his usual, playful grin. He stared at her with determined eyes and a fixed mouth.

Aly nearly tripped. He was there to catch her, his earlier conversation forgotten.

"You are stunning; you know that, right?" He held her upper arms, his bearded face close.

It was the first compliment he'd given her that did not pertain to her magic. As he spoke them, she *craved* the words, the way a child doesn't know her love for honey until first she tries it.

He led her to the dance floor. She was shaking. He might have been too, but Aly couldn't tell over her own jitters. Her heart pounded.

They stood motionless as they awaited the next song. Then they began. His movements were not fluid. He bumped her several times as he tried to direct her steps. She didn't know the dance, and he was clearly out of practice. His frame was stiff, his face almost in a grimace.

"Want to stop?" she asked, her cheeks hot with embarrassment. This had been a bad idea. People near them were chuckling. She wanted to disappear again.

"No." He forced a tight-lipped smile and leaned in closer. "Let them laugh, Aly." His breath lingered on her ear. "While they can."

Whatever that means.

He wasn't graceful, but he held her waist with such delicacy that she wondered if he was afraid to touch her there. When the song ended, Aly was glad—being looked at by so many people was not something she'd mastered yet. Grey, on the other hand, appeared forlorn as they stepped off the dance floor.

As they walked by a group of women chattering, she overheard bits and pieces.

"Apparently his cousin?"

"Grey Manor—"

"Richest man under twenty-five—"

One lady snickered at Aly.

"I might come to regret the cousin story," Grey said with a smirk as they stopped by a display of flowers near the head table.

She wanted this to be simple, but nothing in her life had ever been simple—not her identity, not her magic, not her relationship with Grey.

He still had his hand on the small of her back, so lightly she could barely feel it. "Grey," she began, hoping to be straightforward about what that dance meant. *What did it mean?*

"Hm?" He inched his arm around her, ignoring the pointed looks and whispers all around them.

"Was this a bad idea?"

In answer, he pulled her forehead to his lips and held her there. Her shoulder pressed against his chest; his arm looped across her back. He'd held her that night in the foyer, but she'd been numb. Tonight, she was on fire at his touch.

I promised Mama I'd stay out of the limelight. She inhaled his crisp, familiar smell. Now that she finally understood her mother's keen desire to keep Aly hidden from the world, she found it harder to accept. Grey wasn't exactly a nobody. He was on the king's council. He was a wealthy nobleman of marriageable age. Aly had not thought much of it until this moment, but there had to be dozens of women hoping to win his hand. She'd just never met any of them.

"I should have brought that mask," she whispered.

He pushed back, his hand moving to her upper arm. "No, but I should have known better than to let you wear that dress."

She gave him a small push. "You made it for me!"

"I know." His voice was heavy, his eyes bright against the night.

Just then, a small commotion broke her attention away from Grey. Virienne's king, a dark-skinned man in a pressed white suit that reached to his knees, strode by at a brisk pace with a pair of armed men at his heels. Across his waist was a silver sash that matched his beard, but he had no hair or crown. From one of the armed men, Aly overheard the word "arrival" but nothing else.

The guards had one hand on their revolvers.

Aly shut her eyes and extended her awareness to the magic near her. Grey's Truthwell hummed and pulsed nearly all around her as he stood so close. She wanted to wade into it, that same old temptation present, but she forced her mind to see around it. The young prince's bright energy was somewhere off to the left. Inside, perhaps. The energy from the other guests, all with a Truthwell of their own, clustered in dazzling patches. The stones contained their own small magical Wells, as did the air itself. The ocean far below contained what felt like an endless swath of power, but she passed over it as a possible source. She had Grey, and he was enough.

Then she found what she was looking for. A darkness. She'd never sensed dark magic with her mind before, but she'd assumed it would feel different than the magic present in everything else. Instead of the shimmering, nearly golden threads of energy in the people near her, the magic she now touched was like ash. It skittered away from her, even as her mind sought to explore what it was.

Her fingers tightened around Grey's hand. She hadn't even realized she'd grabbed it.

"What is it?"

But she didn't dare open her eyes, lest she lose the slinking magic. It was trying to *hide* from her, but she didn't know how. Magic couldn't hide from a sorcerer; it was the sorcerer's gift to be able to *see* all the magic in the world.

This was something entirely different. The dark magic slipped away, as if it could pull a shroud over itself. One moment it was there, another moment it was gone.

"There's something here," she whispered, finally giving up and opening her eyes.

The moon shone above and torches lit the night scene. In the dim light, she couldn't see as well as she could with her eyes closed. The magic around her still pulsed, but vision had a way of taking complete control of her mind, blurring the clouds of magic.

Instantly, Grey changed. His body grew rigid, his hands clasped her shoulders. "We must protect the king," he said. "Tell me what you see."

The music still flowed; the glasses still tinkled. Few guests were aware of any threat. Dancers twirled under the stars. Aly searched again for the source of dark magic. She hunted in her mind for the shifting shadow. Each time she felt it, it would slink away. *Could the source of it be moving that fast? How can it know I am looking for it?*

"It's moving quickly," she said. "No human could move like that."

Grey's hand on her cheek was swift and firm. Her eyes popped open, afraid. "Tell me where it is."

She honed in on the darkness once again. "It's coming toward the terrace steps." Fear shone in Grey's eyes. "It's not a person, there's no way."

"A lyth," he hissed.

Lyth. The shape-shifting beast. "No..." Aly's whisper dissolved into the night as Grey turned and jogged toward the table where King Gevar sat with his queen.

As he walked away, terror fixed onto Aly's heart. She hadn't had to travel to the Canyon, after all, to fight the beasts of the Deep.

11

Aly took three deep breaths. "Calm down," she told herself aloud.

A few of the guests had sensed the quick movements, the urgent whispers, the way the Tanderan king and queen were ushered from their table, surrounded by guards.

Think! She needed to protect Grey. That was her duty. But he was beside the king, shuffling his sovereign to safety. Grey was no guard. She didn't know why he was acting like one.

He was a great soldier once, she remembered. Maybe he was the right man to protect the king now.

And I will protect Grey. Aly pulled on Grey's truth, careful to avoid tangling in any of the shadows that twisted among his light. She wasn't sure if it was her panic or if there were *more* shadows in Grey's Truthwell tonight. Using a string of phrases, she constructed a small barrier around him that would at least deflect any direct spells. She had never actually had to defend him—or anyone—from another sorcerer's spellwork before. She had no idea if her magic was properly constructed or how long it would hold against an attack.

"One way to find out," she mused, her hands twisting in the

air in tiny movements as she directed her magic around Grey. The king was so close to Grey. "Might as well include him too." She pulled a little more magic and constructed a barrier around Gevar. She was certain he had a host of protective spells around him already, but she figured another couldn't hurt.

"Stand tall. We have trouble."

Her eyes popped open. No one stood near her, though many milled nearby. A small breeze ruffled the hairs that had fallen beside her face.

A sorcerer. She knew it had to be. Someone had just spoken to her through a shroud. It had been a man's voice. He must have spotted her weaving magic, aware of what her hand movements and mutterings meant.

She nodded firmly to the air; hopeful the man had seen her. Those were the first words a sorcerer had ever said to her.

Without hesitation, she spun toward the place where the darkness lurked, sharpening her mind into needlepoint precision. She conjured up another barrier around Grey and Gevar, but they were moving—walking toward the house—and her protective wall faltered as they strode through it.

"Toss it, Grey!" She wouldn't let him be hurt, not after the way he'd held her just now. Not when she finally knew what she wanted. She shifted the protective barriers and searched again for the moving cloud of ash-dark magic. A lyth could take any animal form, so long as it was not an animal owned or recognized by anyone.

What was a lyth doing here, so far from the Canyon? But if it had traveled as a simple beast, under cover of the forests and fields, a lyth could travel a long way, undetected.

A small, cool breeze indicated her magic had leached power from the air. Other sorcerers were Truthpulling too, and soon frigid air alerted everyone to the real level of the threat.

A woman screamed.

Pandemonium broke loose.

People darted for the stairs, the alcoves, the downstairs entrance to the house. No one knew what to run from or where to run to. One woman tripped, her ankle snapping as she crumpled to the terrace floor.

With a wave of her arms and a heave of air, Aly lifted the woman to her feet, healing her bones as she rose. The woman, dumbstruck, stood trembling in the middle of a current of people. Finally, someone grabbed her arm and pulled her along.

Aly had never seen a living Canyon beast, but the magic it brought with it was easy to hate. The magic of the Deep writhed like a thousand worms, edging out of her awareness as fast as a dissolving fog. With a grunt, Aly yanked on a stone from beneath her feet. The rock cracked, and Aly sucked the power out of it, launching a barrier around herself.

As people scrambled to the perceived safety of the house, Aly's magic felt the prick of a briar. The magic of the Deep had found her.

It's him. She stumbled backward against an ivy-covered wall. *Has my father come here? Has he sent a lyth? Is this my fault?*

Then she saw it. A snake slithered across the stones so quickly it looked like water. Like smoke. It was headed straight for Gevar.

A lyth had no awareness, no ability to pick a target.

At least that's what Aly had always believed.

Her heart dropped out of her chest. This lyth was here for Tandera's king. Grey, who still stood by his sovereign, stepped in front of Gevar. The guards surrounding the king and queen drew their weapons and shuffled the royals toward the house. A shimmering wall of spells caged Gevar and Isabelle—the work of a much more powerful sorcerer. The lyth would never touch them.

But it could hurt Grey.

With a thought that was more instinct than choice, she lifted a hand, pulling up the cobblestones from beneath her feet, and laced them in tight, swirling circles around the snake. People screamed. She smashed the stones together.

When the dust cleared, the tiny form of a mouse scuttled out of the wreckage.

Toss it!

In that moment, a gun fired.

It missed.

Two more bullets missed the scurrying creature. It changed into a cat. Then, as more pistols fired, the creature leaped at the remaining guards, undeterred by Aly's spell shields, and shifted into a man as it collided with the first guard.

Aly trembled in fear. Lyths shouldn't be able to shift into *people!*

She hurled spells at the beast, but it was not affected by them the way a human would be. Its naked form quickly smothered the guard beneath it and grabbed his gun. Grey had a dagger in his hand and the lyth aimed for him. Aly screamed, anchoring herself in Grey's magic and shoving the lyth-man to the ground with a ragged burst of wind that knocked a few of the king's guards down as well.

The creature was on his bare feet in seconds, moving faster than any man should. Before the shocked soldiers could even lunge or shoot, the man turned and bolted. A few bullets missed him as he tossed his gun in the air, shifted from man to leopard, then back to man, grabbing the gun before it hit the terrace.

Aly charged after him, blood flaming in every part of her body. Fear and disgust fused into pure hatred. She would end this creature before it could escape.

The beast whirled and aimed his gun at Grey, as if he knew where Aly was pulling her magic and wanted to cut off her source. In that instant, she plunged into the depths of Grey's Truthwell. As the gun fired, her magic surged, and she slammed the bullet into the terrace floor.

A fierce wind lifted her off the stones, carrying her toward the lyth. In the air, she kicked off her shoes and reached for the nearest thing she could hurl at the now-fleeing jackal. She'd never catch the animal. At least he'd abandoned the gun when he'd taken to four legs.

Aly's arms shook as she held the wind beneath her.

Then she searched with her magic. Stones. The ocean. *Too far*. Window panes. *That could work.*

The jackal raced down a neighboring balcony blanketed with flowering vines. *Vines will do.*

Words trickled from her mouth as she dove deeper into Grey's Truthwell.

The vines responded. They became her tool, completely in her control. The wooden scaffold that held them snapped as the vines pulled free, reaching toward the jackal's ankles.

One tendril looped around the animal's paw. Another caught his chest.

He went down.

In seconds, the vines tangled around the creature's body. The air was ice cold, whipping around Aly with a fierce anger. She was panting with the energy of her magic, unaffected by the cold.

The beast morphed twice as the vines cinched around it. She couldn't tell what form it took, only that the vines wound tighter and tighter as it shrank. Planting her feet on the balcony's banister, Aly shoved her hands apart in the air. The vines smashed together with terrible force.

The darkness vanished.

Heaving air, Aly balanced on the railing and searched the terrace below for signs of the dark magic she'd felt moments ago. It was gone. The tangled vines lay in a heap, a small shape crushed within them.

1 2

As she stepped down onto the patio, Grey's hand on the small of her back was more powerful than the wind that had made her fly.

The few soldiers who remained on the terrace bowed slightly to her. She'd never had anyone bow to her. Her hands shook in Grey's.

He led her across the terrace and into a door under one of the alcoves. No one spoke to her.

Guess my magic is no secret now.

"He'll find me now, won't he?" she whispered as they entered a poorly lit library.

Embers burned low in a hearth. A few guests cowered in the corners. One woman was crying. Grey said nothing and led her quickly down a hallway, trying several handles until he found one that clicked.

They stumbled into a powder room.

He let go of her hand and pushed past her into the small space. Black marble dressed the floor and vanity. Of the six candles in the room, three remained burning. Shadows danced on his face as he spun toward her.

"Are you hurt?" she asked him, ready with her magic to heal any pain inside him.

He shook his head. "You?"

"No."

Several moments passed while Aly took shallow breaths, though her pulse still throbbed. They were in a tiny room, alone. Visions of the warping vines filled her mind, with the memory of the gun aimed at Grey and the shifting form of the leopard-man. She gasped and cupped her hand to her mouth, emotion boiling over. Renna was dead. Her father had killed her. Grey had nearly died. Her magic was no longer a secret. She'd killed a lyth.

Sucking air, she crumpled against the wall.

Grey was there, then she was leaning against him, his hands on her back, her neck, beneath her fallen hair.

His mouth was against her ear. "You saved me tonight. You saved us all."

I wanted to save you. She tried to speak, but she couldn't draw steady breath yet. Her body was exhausted from the concentration and balance she'd used while hovering in the air. As her weight fully hit him, Grey stumbled backward into the vanity, her frame flush against his.

"Aly."

She caught her balance and stepped back. "I'm okay," she said, wiping away tears of shock. This was the second time in two weeks that he'd held her while she cried.

"Aly," he said again, his voice taking on a formal note. "You stopped the bullet. Like it was nothing more than a fly." One finger tilted her chin up. Her body nearly collapsed again at the gentle touch.

She wanted him to lean down, to close the distance between them. She had never expected to like Lord Weston Grey. She had never expected to train as a Master Sorcerer or live among high society either. She hadn't expected to lose her mother without ever seeing her again.

Fresh tears poured down her face, and she turned away. The moment was ruined. She'd destroyed it.

"I feel like I owe you an explanation," Grey said, voice low. He leaned back against his hands. "When I found you, it was for one reason. Not to serve me, but to serve the king."

Her hand, which had been dabbing at tears, stopped and hovered before her shocked face.

"Gevar is in need of a new sorcerer. I can't say much more right now, but I was tasked with finding the best young sorcerer in Tandera and training that person to take the Royal Sorcerer's place. I searched for a year before I found you." He looked down. "I knew you were special that day in Kitrel. I knew you'd be the one to replace the Royal Sorcerer. But I never thought I'd say this." His eyes locked on hers. "I would betray my king to keep you."

Keep you. His words echoed in her ears.

Her wide eyes unsettled him, and he ran a hand through his already messy hair.

Before she could respond, he pushed away from the vanity and grabbed the door handle. "I will set up a meeting with His Majesty as soon as possible. The job, I'm certain, is yours, if you want it." His voice hitched a little at the last phrase.

She could turn it down.

Work for the king. A *Royal* Sorcerer. Three months ago, she was afraid to Truthpull just to ease the pain in her mother's knees. So much had changed. She didn't *have* a mother to comfort anymore.

But she did have a father—*toss him.*

And he would find her soon, now that several witnesses had seen her conjure magic. Just like he'd found out about the bridge, her father would find out about what happened here. He'd come. Grey Manor was no longer her safe haven.

The Royal Sorcerer, on the other hand, was a ghost, a creature few ever saw and fewer still knew. A mystery even among the masked sorcerers.

If her father had killed Renna while trying to find her, he'd kill Grey too. *What if I am not strong enough to stop him?* "My father will come," she said. "He'll come, and if I'm at Grey Manor, he'll kill you. And if I'm not there, I can't protect you."

His hand left the doorknob and found her cheek. "Don't worry about me."

She huffed. "That's not possible."

"I'll find another sorcerer to protect me. Take the job, Aly."

He'd just said he'd betray his king to keep her. He was lying, of course. Weston Grey would no sooner betray his king than Aly would march up to Bulvarna to meet her father.

The day she'd agreed to go with Grey to Mardon was the day he'd promised her to the king, should she prove as powerful as he'd expected. This was the secret he'd harbored.

She wondered why he had just held her like he hadn't intended to say goodbye.

She brushed past him, angry that he'd kept this from her, angry that he'd let her take her walls down. He'd *known* she was training to protect someone else, and he'd still lured her in.

Technically, I asked him to dance tonight, she reminded herself as she stormed back out into the starlit night. Still, he'd accepted.

He'd brought her in here to tell her the truth. Gevar trusted Grey to train her, then give her up. She felt a bit like those paintings hanging in Grey's house: valuable, rare, to be bought by the highest bidder.

Unlike the paintings, however, the final word rested with her.

She could refuse the job.

But she didn't know if she could turn down the *king* and knowingly bring danger to Grey. She didn't know if this strange and unexpected fire between them was enough to warrant that kind of rash behavior.

His hand on her back, his finger tilting her chin, his eyes as they watched her tonight, all were a veneer on top of the truth that he'd planned for Aly to work for the king. Truth was the only thing that mattered.

She would hear the king's offer.

And as they left the seaside estate that night, Aly attempted to convince herself she hadn't yet made up her mind.

13

Augustus Penwater, the aged and dying Royal Sorcerer of Tandera, stared at Aly from behind his red and gold phoenix mask. His cloak, however, was hanging on the rack made especially for it, a large T-shaped wooden stand in the corner of the sorcerer's chambers in Mardon's palace. Rooms that would become Aly's in a few days' time.

She'd made her choice.

Grey had withheld the truth from her. He'd danced with her, only to let her go. Serving the king was the best choice—the safest for Grey and for her.

As a prelude to this all-important job, she had begun a series of meetings with the Royal Sorcerer himself, to learn all manner of wisdom and state secrets from his two-hundred-and-fifteen-year-old mind.

Augustus's power had been waning for years, and the ancient man had finally admitted to the king that he needed a replacement, and soon. His body would simply be too tired to perform magic one day. On that day, he would be useless to the king for protection.

He was the first sorcerer Aly had ever officially met. And he was *the* sorcerer, the best of the best, the Master above all other Masters. The sorcerer supreme.

Aly was taking his place.

It still didn't feel possible. A girl from nowhere, adopted by a nurse, raised in solitude, and brought out of obscurity three months prior.

There was so much she needed to learn, so much she still didn't understand. *Can this man teach it all to me?* His bent frame and wrinkled features, labored breaths and slow movements suggested he might simply stop talking at any moment.

"Magic has kept me spry and upright long enough," he said, an apologetic drawl to his words as he sat, hunched, in his leather arm chair. The man made a rasping sound, and Aly drew to full attention again, rapt at this man's every word, no matter how slowly they came.

"You will find that Binding to one Truthwell is much different than the casual way of magic employed by the Masters." He spoke each word with precision, with effort. He spoke of the elite sorcerers as if they were schoolchildren. "It provides you with a depth of access that no unbound sorcerer can understand. To the others, Binding is a limitation, but I tell you it is not." He slumped a little sideways in the chair.

Aly wondered if she should right him but decided against touching this most untouchable man.

She could not imagine being over two hundred years old, head full of kingdom secrets and histories long forgotten. *What would it even be like to be so tired you couldn't sit up all the way?* Her back stiffened automatically in response, as if grateful it was still able.

From Augustus, she'd learned of the Binding, the magical process by which she would merge her ability to draw power from truth to *one* Truthwell. She could still pull from inhuman objects and creatures, but once Bound, her best and only source of magical energy would be the king.

Once Bound, she could never again pull from Lord Weston Grey.

As if he knew her mind lingered over it, the man asked, "Does it worry you, the Binding?"

"Sir," she began, nervous hands pressing down into her lap, "once Bound to King Gevar, will I be able to sense the other Truthwells?" Grey's Truthwell played its pattern in her mind. He was still waiting in the sitting room downstairs. She could feel it. She couldn't imagine a world devoid of all Truthwells but one.

Augustus drew a rattling breath, making Aly wait. "Ah, the real question, I think, is will you still be able to see Lord Grey's?" For a man barely able to sit up, he saw clearly enough.

Aly blushed crimson. "Truthwells are distracting. How can I learn to pull from only one if I can still sense them all?" The young prince's Truthwell came to mind. His was so bright it was hard to ignore, even though she sat in this room while the prince was shooting skeet out in the gardens. Aly could still touch the luminous magic in that boy as if he were right beside her. Pulling from it would be as easy as curling her fingers into the fabric of her skirt, so close and accessible was the prince's energy.

It was so long before the old man spoke that Aly wondered if she should repeat her question. No one else was in here with them. The king was meeting with an ambassador from Virienne, and he trusted Augustus to tell Aly all she needed to know.

"The truth is attractive to the ones who can see it. Blinding even," he rasped, "once all illusion is removed." She nodded, happy that the man understood. It was so comforting to speak with someone who knew exactly what a Truthwell looked like, what it felt like. "Binding your magic to one person does not stopper your senses to the truth. You will still see Lord Grey's Truthwell." Again, he was cutting right to the chase. "But you will no longer be permitted to pull from it." Augustus progressed through a fit of coughing, as he occasionally did, and when he recovered, he added, "The temptation will always be there, Miss Barron. But you will find that, in time, you will not feel as burdened by it."

Already, she'd mastered the temptation to dive greedily into Grey's Truthwell. His revelation that night at the wedding had been helpful in her ability to quiet the part of her mind that wanted more of him. *I can't want a man that doesn't want me.* He'd lied, of course, when he'd said he would betray Gevar and keep her talent a secret from the king.

Her initial overpowering desire to consume all the energy in his beautiful Truthwell was mortifying and childish, though it was still there. That was what it was to become a Master, to draw energy from the truth without choking on it in ravenous consumption.

A thought occurred to her. "You must still sense the Truthwells of the staff and royal family?" *Is the prince's light as distracting to him as it is to me?*

He gave a small, jerking nod. "They are nothing more than stars in my sky."

"The prince? His Truthwell isn't bright to you?" If this man could learn to ignore the prince's brightness, she could too. That was a comfort.

"There is but one Truthwell that no sorcerer, Bound or not, can ignore."

Aly perked up. The heat from the fire was roasting her right side, but the man across from her had a blanket on his lap. His magic must not be able to keep him warm anymore.

"If you ever come across a source that appears as white as the sun at midday, if its light burns you to observe it directly"— Aly's heart knotted as he spoke— "then you, perhaps, have found what is called a Beacon."

"Beacon, sir?"

He coughed again, a rattling, ugly sound. "It is a rarity even among Masters. But there are enough historical records to believe it does happen. A Beacon is a man or woman whose Truthwell calls to a particular sorcerer. The truth calls to us all, but a Beacon, as history and mythology dictate, has a purpose to fulfill. If you ask me, the truth has a purpose, no matter if it shines more brightly in one person than another. I have never seen a Beacon, though perhaps that was because in my two-hundred-some-odd years, Theod did not see fit to make me a Beholder. That, or it is simply because the world was somewhat stationary. Beacons have only been documented to occur at what we later recognize as pivotal moments in the world's unfolding."

His words filled the warm room, stoking the heat in Aly's cheeks to a stifling degree. *Could the prince be a Beacon? Why, if they were so rare, would she of all people be able to see one? And what was pivotal about* her *life?*

Perhaps she was mistaken. She was still so new to Truth-pulling, maybe it was that she'd never encountered a bright Truthwell before. A Beacon, surely, was something else entirely. Unmistakable. *Like the sun at midday*, he'd said.

As Augustus lifted a hand, dismissing her, he pushed back his mask, revealing a deeply wrinkled brown face, week-old stubble, and drooping yet lively brown eyes. "It seems as if the world rests for periods of about two or three hundred years. Then something happens. I would not be at all surprised if a Beacon existed in the world right now." The skin around his eyes crinkled. "The sorcerer who can see it is the sorcerer who will change the world."

∾

A week later, Aly, alongside Grey, was leaving the warmth of the king's personal study when a small knot clogged her throat. Augustus had died in his sleep the night before.

It was now her turn to stand beside the king.

She'd learned all she could from the old man. It would have to be enough.

The wealth and power displayed even in the hallways of the palace still impressed Aly, though the initial shock of it all had worn off. Intricate parquet floors peeked out beneath the silvery threads of rugs from across the great ocean. The hand-carved crown molding was plaited with pure gold. So different from her cabin in the woods.

Home. This was Aly's new home.

Enormous oil paintings of the king's family lined the walls. From one painting, the young prince stared at her as she passed. Without having to think about it, she knew exactly where the prince was at every moment. His blindingly bright Truthwell never left the corners of her consciousness.

She planned to study the history of Beacons, but at her core, she still did not think it could be as Augustus had said. If the world needed changing, she wouldn't be the one to do it.

Ignoring the pull of the prince's distant energy, she listened to Grey's breaths and footsteps beside her. The magic in him, while not as bright as Prince Frederick's, had become a familiar song—one she would never again sing.

He would leave, and she would stay.

A thin band of smoke twisted around the middle finger on her left hand. The ring of a Master. A bit of ash swirled in the tiny, black band. She'd been cautious of making the ring, knowing it was used as a means of lifting oneself above others— much like a crown. But while she *did* wear her ring with the pride of reaching a lofty goal, she wore hers also for a different reason: as a reminder of *why* she'd reached Mastery—because in her blood ran both power and fear. Her father was still searching for her. The ring was her way of proving to herself that she could survive Dimitri Patrenko, when their paths finally crossed.

She vowed to wear the black ring until her father was no longer a threat. Then, perhaps, she might change the ring into something prettier.

Glancing at the ring, she still couldn't fully believe she was Tandera's Royal Sorcerer, official now that she had Bound to the king in the hours after Augustus' death. The ceremony had taken place in secret, with no one but Gevar and Isabelle in attendance. The fewer people who knew of the change in Royal Sorcerer, the better.

The king had been kind to Aly after the wedding, offering his thanks for her protection that night. When he'd learned of her mother's death, he'd even given her an enormous hug. He was not as stuffy as she'd first imagined. He was worth protecting. Tandera loved him, and Tandera needed him.

Somehow, she was the one given the chance to serve the king. The girl who'd been afraid of the magic inside her now wore the ring of a Master. The red and gold phoenix mask of the Royal Sorcerer covered her face as they walked into the palace foyer.

At the top of the grand stair leading down into the marbled space, Aly stopped. Grey knew his way out. Here they would part.

Her chest ached as she stared at Grey.

"It was always going to be you," he said, hands in his suit pockets. She wanted him to reach out, but they both knew it would be pointless. Part of her hated that he'd ever touched her. Part of her would cherish forever the memory of their dance, of the way he'd looked at her in that powder room. "You will be the best sorcerer this nation has ever seen."

She scoffed. "Augustus had two hundred years on me. I don't know if I'll ever be as good as he once was." *Or as good as my father is.* As Royal Sorcerer, she would, at some point, likely travel to her father's country. What would she do then? How could she convince Gevar to stay away from the country to the north?

Problems for another day. For now, the safest place—and the place where she would grow strongest—was beside the king.

Grey looked down. "You'll live a long time too."

Aly couldn't conceive of ever reaching two hundred years in age.

With a deep breath, Aly reminded herself of something she'd come to accept: Marriage would not be for her. As a girl, she'd feared her magic, thinking a man would revile her for it. Now, as Royal Sorcerer, she would be forever unapproachable, forever in the margins of history, a shield of shadow for the king. As a Master Sorcerer, she could expect to live double the lifespan of an average person; another reason no man would ever want her.

To live that long, even without the mask of secrecy she now would wear, was to live alone. She labored to rebuild the walls around her heart that would keep the loneliness at bay for what could be a *very* long life.

Grey had been a ray of hope, the first and only time she'd thought someone could know the depth of her magic and still want her. But it had all been a play. He'd known the curtain would fall and end their charade, but he'd let it happen anyway. She wanted to hate him for it, for the way her heart hurt as he stood there saying goodbye.

"You taught me much, Alyana Barron. Grey Manor will be darker without you."

She didn't have the strength to say what was on her mind. She nodded and watched him descend the marble steps. On the edges of her mind, she sensed the prince moving in the palace, getting closer. She had to shut her mind against him. As Royal Sorcerer, Aly was here for Gevar, and, no matter the effort it took, she would learn to ignore the prince's Truthwell. She would also learn to ignore Grey's.

"Grey," she rasped.

He spun back.

If she didn't say something to him now, she never would. "Thank you." *For teaching me. For dancing with me. For finding me.* "For this. I will be safe here. At least for now." *And you promised to keep me safe.* Now that she was Bound to the king, she no longer had the right to speak to Grey's mind. She hoped her tone said what her words did not.

The country would remain uninformed of the change of sorcerers. She would spend most of her time invisible; in public, Aly would wear Augustus's red and gold mask. She would wear tall shoes with her sorcerer's cloak. Those who'd seen her at the wedding were told that Grey's young, magical cousin was hired as a Protector by Virienne royalty. The lie was such that, when said in a certain way, wasn't actually false: Aly *was* hired to protect royalty. And Aly wouldn't be the one forced to speak the half-truth, so her magic wouldn't become tainted with the lie. Some rumors circulated that the young girl was sent away by the stone-hearted Lord Grey, who'd been embarrassed by the way she'd acted around him at the wedding. What people believed was neither Aly's nor Grey's concern.

Either way, Grey and Gevar were convinced that Aly's father would not trace her back to the palace in Mardon.

In this way, Alyana Barron would disappear from the world.

At least, for a time. Aly knew she would one day meet her father, face to face. Two Royal Sorcerers; one infected by the magic of the Deep, the other a novice, albeit born with strength. When that day came, she would not go down without a fight.

"Goodbye, Aly," Grey said. "I know the Royal Sorcerer isn't supposed to speak to anyone but the king, but if you ever want to rehash all those times you knocked me over in the field, I'd be happy to oblige."

She smiled and held back a laugh. "I'll remember that." She would have to see him every time he came to visit Gevar. See but not be seen. One day, down the road, whenever he found a woman to marry, she'd probably attend the wedding with Gevar.

For a minute there, I thought it might work, she said to herself, wishing he could hear, but not wanting to say it aloud. Never in her long years of existence would Aly ever let herself think something so foolish again.

Just then, the young prince's Truthwell flared against Aly's senses, causing her to shudder. In seconds, he burst through the foyer below, his oldest sister tailing him, shouting at him to give something back. Grey turned and chuckled at the scene, but when he turned back to Aly, he pinned her with a piercing look.

"He's that bright, is he?" asked Grey, observing Aly's squinting expression.

He remembered her words. She offered a faint nod and steeled her mind. The prince, if Theod willed it, would be king one day, and Aly would serve him. Until that day, she would have only one Truthwell to pull from: King Gevar's. Beacon or not, and she assumed not, the prince wasn't the one she was Bound to.

Before her, the energy swirling in Lord Weston Grey was full of both light and shadow, the patterns woven as intricately as an ancient tapestry. She understood now what some of his shadows represented. Ondorian had said not all secrets were lies, but the shadows in Grey's Truthwell were the kind of secrets that concealed the truth, the kind of secrets that brought darkness with them.

She closed her eyes and, for a moment, let his energy crash around her. Though she still longed to use it all at once, she'd learned to withstand the sensation. When she opened her eyes, she closed her mind to his Truthwell. His light was off limits now. Forever.

"Aly, I wasn't planning to tell you, but you'll hear it soon enough anyway," said Grey. "I signed up for another tour at the Canyon. Three years, then I can decide if I want to come home."

Her heart pinched painfully inside her. "Giving up your place on the council?"

"Not exactly. Gevar said I could return to it whenever I wanted it. He's a good man. I'm glad you'll be the one protecting him."

"And your late-night meetings? I know what you do, Grey." Augustus Penwater, collector of secrets, had told her in one of their meetings.

His face betrayed his shock only in a quick blink and the flexing of his jaw. "Someone else will do it. The king has many willing hands."

"But few who are as good at secrets, I'm sure."

He let out an annoyed laugh. "Surely you see why the king bid me keep that work a secret."

Aly nodded. "Illegal shipping and trade. Definitely worth keeping under wraps. What's interesting is that the king required it of you at all."

Now he smiled. "You have a lot to learn about the business of kings."

Not sure how to respond to that, Aly thought back to what Grey had just told her. "So you were lying when you said we could rehash all those times my magic knocked you down." *The man is full of lies. The little ones, the ones that hurt.*

He stared up at her, a fleeting darkness washing over his features. "I had something sent to your rooms. I hope you like it." He nodded once, lips pressed together, and then left the palace.

"Goodbye, Grey," she whispered. Then she pulled her shroud around her body and slipped from view.

∼

In her room, a painting by Umberto Yvsey was propped against a large wooden desk. It was a still of a vase filled with peonies.

A note on the desk read, *Because I never got the chance to give you flowers.*

∼

To read the backstory on Weston Grey, click here for exclusive access to Mask of Secrets, or go to vip.cfeblack.com/join.

ALSO BY C. F. E. BLACK

Scepter and Crown Series:

Blade of Ash - Scepter and Crown Book One

Crown of Dust - Scepter and Crown Book Two

Scepter of Fire - Coming Soon!

Other Titles:

The Veritas Project

If you enjoyed this book, please consider leaving a quick review. They help more than you know.

Continue reading for a sneak peek at Blade of Ash!

ACKNOWLEDGMENTS

First, thank you to my tribe of readers who've loved this book since it was handed out to all my first fans. I wrote it entirely for you, and I'm so glad you love Weston Grey as much as I do.

Also, I have to thank my husband, who didn't think I was weird when I started walking around the yard, talking into my phone (and eventually microphone) to create my stories. Your support means everything.

To Dad, for sitting with me at that birthday party and helping me iron out the plot, and Mom, for your ceaseless cheerleading.

To my editor, Monica, for making this book smooth and easy to read.

To Damian, for starting something amazing with this first cover.

To all the readers who find this book, thank you for taking the time to read my story.

And to you, Lord, for making this writer journey possible. As with all things, soli Deo gloria.

ABOUT THE AUTHOR

C. F. E. Black loves to get swept away in books, both reading and writing them. Fantasy and science fiction have been her bread and butter since childhood, and she can't imagine life without her beloved fictional worlds. She lives in beautiful north Alabama with her superhero husband, sons, and fur-family. Connect with her and find free stories at www.cfeblack.com.

BLADE OF ASH

• SCEPTER AND CROWN BOOK ONE •

C. F. E. BLACK

HILLCITY PRESS

1

RED

Doors didn't often bother Prince Frederick, nor did they give him headaches or drag him out of bed after a restless night. But this wasn't just any door. Of all five hundred twenty-seven doors in the palace, this was the only one he had not been permitted to enter. Ever.

Or rather, that had been the rule before Frederick's father died.

Working up the courage to say what he'd spent half the night rehearsing in his head, the prince, groggy and puffy eyed from grief, stared at the Royal Sorcerer's door. The shock of his father's passing was still a raw, wide wound, muddying his thoughts.

Today, when the world would turn their tear-stained faces upon the crown prince for guidance, when he had a million other tasks to accomplish, a million other issues to think about, here he was, trying for the hundredth time to open this door.

The gray wood carved with delicate patterns and covered in tiny shadows hinted at the magic hidden behind it, the magic that he'd once envied—the magic that should have kept his father alive.

Frederick swatted a curl off his forehead and checked the corridor for watching eyes; he saw none but the silent faces on the paintings, then stepped closer to the knob. He lifted his chin and pounded his fist against the door; he was reduced to *knocking* on the door that, in his opinion, had kept him from his father far too often.

Many conversations with his father had ended at this door. As a child, he'd raced down the long palace corridors after the king. As he had grown older, he'd walked the halls alongside his father, discussing matters of state or one of Carolyn's new inventions.

Their talks had always ended here. *It is for your safety that you must leave the sorcerer alone, until it is your time,* his father would say, choosing, as always, the sorcerer's secrecy over his own son's curiosity.

Sadness, sudden and overwhelming, clawed at Frederick's chest.

No one in the palace—in all Tandera—had authority over him now, not even this door. The king was not here anymore to chastise Frederick for attempting a peek at the mysterious sorcerer.

Frederick shook away his sadness and knocked again, louder. "You can't shut me out now!" he yelled, his fist smearing down the doorframe with a pathetic squeak.

With his father's final breath, Frederick had inherited the throne of this nation, but his title as king would not be official until he was Bound to the Royal Sorcerer. However, as Theod would have it, the prince had been asleep when his father had passed and the country slipped quietly onto Frederick's shoulders, and despite the oaths he'd muttered, trembling in shock, one hand resting on an ancient copy of the *Verad* just after midnight, the reality of his new position hadn't really sunk in.

King.

King Frederick.

It didn't sound right. Not yet. This wasn't supposed to happen to him for *years*.

He wouldn't hold his first council meeting as king until after the Accession Ceremony, when he would publicly say the vows and hold the scepter and, at age eighteen, become one of Tandera's youngest sovereigns. But the throne was his, and with the throne came the magic of the Royal Sorcerer—the man who'd *killed* his father. Or let him die. Same difference.

The sorcerer, powerful enough to stop a bullet in the air, had not stopped the disease that had begun to drain Frederick's father's health three months ago. No one had expected it to take the king's life.

Bells chimed in the distance. The call to mourning had begun. All across the city, people woke to the news of their sovereign's death. Obediently, they would step out of their homes, open their windows, or stand on their rooftops, glass jars in hand, rattling the coins inside—a way of remembering the fallen king who had been a good leader, his reign a prosperous one for all of Tandera. The coins were the evidence. Even from the palace, nestled among its vast gardens, the sound was sublime.

As the noise coaxed up a fresh wave of tears, the prince couldn't help but peer out the window at the end of the hall. For the first day in a week, it was sunny, despite the early spring rains he could see hovering outside the city. The sorcerers of Mardon were performing their part in the ritual of mourning; it took a city's worth of sorcerers to hold back the rain.

Frederick clunked his head against the doorframe. Determination kept him from succumbing to the exhaustion of grief.

With a frown, he tried the knob.

It didn't budge.

The prince's face grew warm, his anger rising. The man who lived in these rooms—forever hidden behind cloak and mask to all but the king—had some explaining to do, and Frederick would speak to him, now, even if it meant taking an axe to the handle.

"This is absurd," he said into the empty hall. He understood, at least in part, being denied entrance while his father had still lived, but not now.

A creak behind him preceded Sebastian Thorin's deep voice. "Did you try the handle, halfwit?"

With a start, Frederick called out, with a hint of a smirk, "Yes, you idiot. What are you doing here?"

Seb strolled into the hall, still in his nightshirt, but wearing pants that looked as if he'd had them on for days. "Whole palace is looking for you." He grinned, his dark skin still sheet-creased.

A weight dropped in Frederick's gut. The entire country of Tandera was looking to him now, and he wasn't sure he could be who they wanted. They wanted to see his father, King Gevar, but they'd have to settle for Frederick.

"But those fools thought you might be in the garden or the solarium or some nonsense." Seb's bright smile lessened the weight inside Frederick. "No, I knew you were stupid enough to come here first. And you still can't get in!" Echoes of his cackling laugh bounced down the hallway.

Though anyone else would consider the day after the king's death the worst day to laugh at Frederick, Sebastian Thorin thought it was the perfect day for it, and this was why Frederick liked him better than the other young people who tiptoed around the prince like he had to be handled as delicately as a cocked pistol.

"I can have you hanged," Frederick threatened.

"Then who else would dare you to do stupid things?"

"Fortunately, no one."

"And that would be boring." Seb stepped up to the sorcerer's door. "Let's have a look." He never asked why Frederick was here instead of downstairs eating breakfast or rehearsing his lines for the public address he had to give later. "Hinges would be easy enough to blow. Want me to work something up?"

"We can't blow the door down. It's *magic*, remember?"

Seb shrugged. "Well, it's one thing we haven't tried yet, and I'm getting better at smaller explosions."

Frederick laughed. It felt wonderful. "You said that last time and nearly blew up half the garden." For the briefest moment, he forgot that his father would never wake.

"But those gophers got what was coming to them. No more tunnels under the roses."

"No more roses."

"Small matter."

The memory faded along with Frederick's smile. "Well, as long as you're standing here, of course the door won't open. Hiding just out of sight doesn't work. Tried it several times with Father."

Seb lifted his hands in surrender and walked toward the stairwell. "What will you say to him?"

Frederick had considered this in the silent hours after his father had died. "I'll demand an answer." Frederick cracked his knuckles. "A Reckoning."

Seb's easy smile faltered. "You think he's responsible, don't you?"

"My father should still be alive."

"Yes, he should." Seb had the decency to say nothing for a moment.

In the silence, the two stared at the nearest mural. In it, a vast, shadowy canyon stretched out before lines of soldiers on horseback. Shadows seemed to creep out of the earth, some in the shape of hands and others appearing to have eyes. At the head of the troops of mounted soldiers, a king rode atop a black horse. Beside him stood a masked figure in a white cloak—the sorcerer.

Finally, Seb said, "Brother, if you request a Reckoning, all that will do is prove you don't trust him—not a great way to start your reign. Their magic comes from the *truth*. Sorcerers don't tell lies."

With one knuckle, Frederick tapped the painting, right over the heart of the shadowy depths. "Some do."

Seb didn't argue that. Instead, he shrugged and scratched his day-old beard. "Let's make a bet."

Frederick waved him away. "Just leave. Please."

"Hear me out: If the guy has facial tentacles, I win. If he has warts or boils, you win."

Despite the tremor of fear in his stomach and the grief still clutching at his throat, Frederick forced a laugh. "That's a terrible bet. I never even said he *has* boils."

"He wears the mask for *some* reason."

"They all do. Now, please leave." Frederick's anger had subsided with Seb's presence, but the bitter reality was that his father's body was off to the mortician to be cleansed and dressed and prepped for his pyre. "Go. Tell Bernard and Yin and the others that I will be at breakfast shortly."

He watched his friend depart. When he turned back around, the sorcerer's door was ajar.

"Come in," a female voice said.

He was suddenly furious that the sorcerer had an *attendant* who was allowed in here. Frederick stepped in and shut the door behind him. The room, one he'd painted in his mind countless times, was nothing spectacular. No jars of preserved creatures like Seb had postulated. No bizarre apparatus to cage powerful men should they become unruly. All the theories, all the dreams, evaporated as Frederick observed a sitting room, complete with two leather chairs; a soot-stained fireplace; a vibrant rug; even a painting of flowers that boasted the signature of Umberto Yvesy, one of Tandera's most popular artists. So the sorcerer liked art.

Flowers? He'd not imagined a gnarled old man to appreciate a still of peonies.

Frederick glanced around for the attendant who had welcomed him. He opened his mouth to voice his annoyance when a woman suddenly *materialized.*

At a small desk by the latticed window, she shuffled papers, in a bit of a frenzy.

For several seconds he stared at her. She had not been standing there a moment ago. Bright sunlight painted a glow around her profile. She never looked at him, as if his presence were secondary to whatever was on those loose pages. She wore a plain red dress, belted, and was barefoot.

She turned a curious expression on him. Eyebrows lifted, head tilted, she waited for him to speak.

He could not. His gaze traveled to her feet, perhaps a little too slowly, and back up to her narrow, slightly freckled face.

She sniffed, annoyed with his examination of her.

"My king," she said with a sweeping curtsey, her voice now infused with adoration—mock or reverent, he didn't know. The look on her face when she straightened, however, suggested the former. She placed two hands on her hips. "Okay, stop gaping. You've seen me now." She waved both hands through the air in frustration or embarrassment. "Want me to be invisible again?"

The crown prince cleared his throat. "Everyone says sorcer*er*, not sorcer*ess*." He could not accept that this…young woman was the almighty sorcerer he'd imagined his entire life. He knew sorcerers could be women, but he had been *certain* Tandera's was a man. The broad-shoulders of the cloak. The rather manly phoenix mask. She looked *shorter* than the figure who'd stood by his father's side. Surely, the sorcerer was having fun with him on his first day. *Could the man change his appearance? He can make himself invisible, why not make himself look like an attractive woman?*

The woman walked toward him, her bare feet making small

slapping sounds on the parquet.

"A woman can be a pain*ter*; a woman can be a law*yer*; a woman can be a cobb*ler*, a farm*er*, a hunt*er.*"

"But—"

"*Er!*" she snapped, lips pursing at the syllable.

Frederick temporarily forgot he still thought there was a man somewhere underneath this disguise. She stood a few feet away, staring up at him, brown hair braided, her green eyes hard, her mouth a slim line. She had no jesting in her expression.

His shoulders sank with a breath.

"Have we come 'round?" She strode back to the desk strewn with papers and shifted more pages with long fingers.

Frederick stole another glance at the rest of her, his throat and his chest trying to shrink into one another.

This was not good.

How can this young woman be my sorcerer?

No. Not good at all.

How could she have been the sorcerer that served my father? The one who'd let him die.

All his questions slammed into him at once, but the most desperate one surfaced first. "Why?"

It was more of a croak than an actual word, but by the horrified look on her face, she'd heard him and understood.

Instead of answering, she pulled one paper out of the mess and held it against her for a moment, as if it contained a secret spell that, once revealed, would expose her true identity as some moth-eaten ancient corpse. Absently, she slid the paper down one side of her body, the *shh* sound of it drawing Frederick's eye.

"We have much to discuss." She adopted a more official tone and moved toward one of the two high-back leather chairs before the fireplace. No fire today, only a pile of gray and black ash. "Sit." She plopped unceremoniously into one chair and immediately pulled her bare feet into her lap, crossing her legs and arranging the folds of her dress to hang down around her. This made her look even younger. His age, even.

Frederick swallowed, still waiting for her to answer his question, and took a seat. He ran one finger around the collar of his tight jacket.

In a casual tone, she said, "Take that thing off if you like."

He gawked at her, then realized this wasn't that strange a remark. After all, he could remove his jacket while in the presence of his family and closest friends. She was his secret body guard, his greatest weapon. No one else would ever join them in these conferences.

He left the jacket buttoned to the top.

"Your Majesty, I know you have questions. Ask away." She left the paper in her lap and spread her arms wide in a gesture that felt strangely intimate to Frederick, who was used to the women of court barely moving in his presence as they attempted to look poised. Only his sisters had ever made grand gestures around him.

For a moment, he panicked and wondered if she could read his thoughts. Better to know that now. "Can you read my mind?" he blurted, a little too forcefully.

She laughed. He wasn't used to strange women laughing at him.

"No. Magic can do many things, including invade someone's head, but it can't bring back what it finds there. And I have absolutely *no* desire to see what's in your head." She glanced down, possibly hiding a brief flush on her cheeks, as if nervous. "Next question."

He swallowed an unwelcome lump in his throat. "My father."

Fortunately, she seemed to have been anticipating this turn of conversation. She lifted the sheet of paper toward Frederick. He was alarmed to see she was fighting tears.

He began to read.

My King,

I know you are heartbroken over your loss. King Gevar was nothing but noble and deserved to live longer. From the bottom of my heart, I ask that you forgive me. I have studied my art for years, but nothing in my powers could save him. I tried.

I will miss him terribly.

There was no closing, no name. Frederick glanced up at the woman, who now swabbed at tears with both hands. She cried without sound. He sat there watching her, the letter of apology in his hand. She was *crying*. His sorcerer supreme was crying.

"You were...close with my father?" The venom in his tone did not escape her notice.

"Oh! Nothing like that! He was like a..." Her words fell away. "I never knew my father." For a moment, a shadow passed over her face. "Gevar was so kind. So strong."

Frederick nodded. "He was indeed. And he died before his time." *Thanks to your incompetence.* Frederick glanced back at the letter then again at his sorcerer. "You said you tried?"

"Yes, I tried," she snapped.

"But you're a sorce*rer*."

"Oh, and that makes me, what? Perfect?" She looked away, toward the ashes.

He didn't know how to respond. She was supposed to protect the king, to keep him alive. For three agonizing months something had eaten away at his father's bones and organs to the point that Gevar had been in pain everywhere.

Frederick stood and tossed the apology paper onto the chair. "You expect me to accept that? Explain what—"

"Your father was cursed," she interrupted.

His mouth froze, half open.

She watched him, arms crossed, as if she wanted to hide behind them. "Yes. A death curse."

Inside of Frederick, his throat gnarled into a labyrinth, and his words could not escape. At last, he managed, "How can I trust you?"

She stood with a huff. Her face was narrow and smooth. She wore no color on her eyes or cheeks or lips like the women he encountered at court. Her green eyes were fierce, as if she too fought back buried anger. "Look, I know you blame me. I blame myself!" More tears filled her eyes. "But a death curse is different. There was only one way to heal Gevar, and he—"

"There was a way to heal him?" he balked.

The woman never faltered or stepped back. "He made me promise not to."

"I don't believe you."

"I tried to stop the curse. I *did* slow it, but once a curse like that is activated, there are only two known ways to heal a death curse. One is to cast it back into the sorcerer who created it—an impossibility in this case—and the other is to perform an act called siphoning." Her hands fumbled with the fabric of her dress. "Siphoning draws magic out of one person and into another. Papa made me promise not to do it."

Papa? Frederick's mouth hardened like clay in a kiln. She fidgeted with her pockets. *I called him Father. Who is* she *to have called him Papa?* Jealousy, furious and wild, roared within Frederick.

"You could have lied," he hissed.

"No!" Her face paled. "I couldn't lie!"

"You could have saved him! Just one lie and my father would be alive!" He'd taken another step toward her. They were close, breathing heavy. Maddeningly, she smelled lovely. Like lavender. Frederick was not backing down first. *She* was to blame for the king's death. She admitted it. She could not expect him to trust her.

Finally, she pressed her hands to her face and exhaled loudly. When she looked at him again, her eyes were rimmed in tears, but her mouth was hard. "Do you know what siphoning does?"

Before he could respond, she continued, "Like I said, to perform that act, I would have had to take the curse into myself. I *wanted* to. I begged him to let me do it!" She shook her head. "But your father knew that if *I* became cursed, I'd end up like..." Her words broke off. She lifted her chin. "Like the sorcerers who trust the Deep. And he did not want to risk what would happen if someone like me became cursed with the Canyon's magic."

"So it's okay for a king to be cursed, just not you?"

Her lips pinched into a tight frown. "No, it's not okay, Your Majesty."

The title sounded strange to Frederick, and more so coming from this woman who'd been yelling at him a moment ago.

He stared out the window, breathing hard, his mind pinwheeling with this new information. A death curse. *Who would curse a king? Why?* This was the sort of news that could start a war.

As these questions volleyed in his thoughts, he became aware that she stood behind him, waiting. His skin prickled. She was going to try to Bind to him.

He'd known this moment would come. His whole life, he'd anticipated it. Binding his Truthwell to the power of the Royal Sorcerer was an action every king had performed—as ritualistic and predictable as the coronation ceremony. Yet he'd expected to Bind to a wizened old man. He'd expected to Bind much later in life. He'd expected...toss it all, he'd expected to *want* to Bind when the time came.

"I will *not* Bind to the person responsible for my father's death," he said, voice flat and firm as he whirled on her.

Her face was wet with tears, but she ignored them, letting them drip off her chin. In her eyes, a seething anger brewed. "You spoiled little..."

"Finish that sentence and you'll be finding a new royal to serve."

His thoughts buzzed with the stupidity of his words—she

knew as well as he did that he couldn't *fire* the Royal Sorcerer. She'd served the kingdom for too long, knew too many state secrets, and had, by Theod's great design, been gifted with magic much stronger than the average sorcerer. But he couldn't back down now. He'd lost a father. She'd lost...her employer, regardless of what she called him.

In the wake of his words, her chest heaved up and down, her nostrils flaring as she discarded response after response that flashed across her face. Words weren't necessary to communicate what was on her mind. Rage. Offense. Hurt. Desperation.

He'd not expected that last one. To force himself to look away, he tugged at his jacket's sleeves.

Finally, after one long exhale, she said, "I know you don't trust me, but we have to do this."

That hadn't been what he'd expected her to say. She was capitulating—bowing out of the fight. He detected a note of panic in her voice.

"You're to be king now, and it's the only way to keep you safe." She offered a deferential nod.

"Wait." It couldn't be that simple. For a moment there, she'd looked ready to dismember him with her magic. He straightened his spine. "I demand a Reckoning first."

Her eyes narrowed. "How *dare* you." With a jerking movement, she spun toward the door, fumes of anger reeling off her like smoke from a freight train.

That was easy, Frederick thought, marching after her. "Right now?"

"Yes, right now." From a rack beside the door, she ripped down her white sorcerer's cloak and yanked her phoenix mask off a hook on the wall. "Ondorian is still in the palace."

"And how do you know that?"

Over her shoulder, she said, "I see everyone's Truthwell. I know his, just like I know your sisters', your mother's, and yours." She closed her eyes. "He's in the chapel. Let's go."